"Hot" and "hockey mom" had never connected for him before. Not until Clare.

In all his years watching his daughter play hockey, Bryan had never once noticed how good another player's mom looked in jeans. He'd never wondered how hot she'd look if he had the chance to see her in a skirt—or out of a skirt, for that matter. Now he couldn't be near Clare for five minutes before his thoughts skated down paths they hadn't taken since he got married...or since the divorce.

He looked back at the action on the ice. He was not, under any circumstances, going to let himself think about Clare that way again. They had to get along to help the kids through this mediation thing.

And he'd be willing to bet the counselor didn't expect them to sleep together as part of the deal.

Dear Reader,

I wrote the first scene of this book long before I knew exactly what the story would be about. I had an idea for a dad and a daughter he loved fiercely but couldn't quite connect with, and from that scene grew *Calling the Shots*.

I love to write about the complicated, messy side of relationships. In the book Clare says that she can't trust herself and I can relate to that idea. How do lovers, or even parents and children, move past the fears and doubts that get in the way of satisfying connections? How does anyone have the courage to try again when they've been badly hurt in the past? When is it worth taking a risk and when is it smarter to run?

I hope you'll enjoy reading along as Bryan and Clare wrestle with these issues.

Extras, including behind-the-scenes facts, deleted scenes and information about my other books are on my Web site, www.ellenhartman.com. Look for other Harlequin Superromance authors and readers on our Facebook page at www.facebook.com/ HarlequinSuperromance. I'd love to hear from you! Send e-mail to ellen@ellenhartman.com.

Happy reading!

Ellen Hartman

Calling the Shots
Ellen Hartman

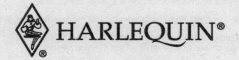

TORONTO • NEW YORK • LONDON
AMSTERDAM • PARIS • SYDNEY • HAMBURG
STOCKHOLM • ATHENS • TOKYO • MILAN • MADRID
PRAGUE • WARSAW • BUDAPEST • AUCKLAND

Recycling programs
for this product may
not exist in your area.

ISBN-13: 978-0-373-71665-4

CALLING THE SHOTS

www.eHarlequin.com

Printed in U.S.A.

ABOUT THE AUTHOR

Ellen grew up in Pennsylvania where she played many sports including baseball, basketball and track. (Her efforts for the cross-country team were more comical than athletic.) After graduating from Carnegie Mellon with a degree in creative writing, she spent the next fifteen years writing technical documentation. Eventually, she worked up the courage to try fiction and has been enjoying her new career as a romance author.

Currently Ellen lives in a college town in New York. She and her husband spend much of their free time watching their sons play baseball, soccer and, of course, hockey.

Books by Ellen Hartman

HARLEQUIN SUPERROMANCE
1427—WANTED MAN
1491—HIS SECRET PAST
1563—THE BOYFRIEND'S BACK
1603—PLAN B: BOYFRIEND

This book is dedicated to the parents and volunteers who share their time, talent and enthusiasm with kids through youth sports, especially my brother, Jerry.

In his first outing as a stand-in coach, he led our sister's basketball team to their only "almost-win" of the season. The story of that game is a family favorite!

I would also like to thank the parents of the Ithaca Youth Hockey Squirt travel team who answered my questions about hockey terms and technique. Chris Thomas was especially helpful, and I regret that I wasn't able to include some of his hilarious cheers in the book.

Finally, I continue to rely on the expertise and support of my critique partners, Diana, Harriett, Leslie, Liz and Mary. They were particularly helpful at the beginning of this project when Tim underwent a much-needed personality makeover.

CHAPTER ONE

BRYAN WAS BEYOND LATE. He'd missed Allie's entire practice. He just hoped she was still at the rink. He'd texted her, but she hadn't replied. His sister, who watched Allie when he was gone, wasn't picking up, either.

Not good.

So not good. People weren't almost an hour late to pick up their thirteen-year-old kids from hockey. At least not people who were good at being parents.

He was going to have to arrange a backup plan for the nights he was coming from out of town. One more arrangement to get this whole precarious mess he and Allie were calling a family under control.

He sure as hell hoped Erin's new life was worth it.

He pulled into the drop-off circle at the front of the rink. It was past nine o'clock—no one was going to complain if he left the Lexus there for a few minutes.

He took the stairs three at a time, his bad knee twinging as he landed on the icy top step, but he ignored the old pain. Bryan yanked the doors open, the blast of warmth hitting him hard after the bitter cold air. He was already scanning the lobby, checking the worn, tweed couches for his daughter when Danny Jackson, the rink manager, popped his head out of his office.

"Bryan," Danny said. "I need to talk to you."

Bryan glanced over but kept walking toward the

locker rooms. "I'll be back in one sec. I'm late picking up Allie," he called. She wasn't in the lobby but she had to be here somewhere. She wouldn't have asked someone to drop her at the apartment. Not when she knew he was out of town.

"There was a fight, Bry," Danny said. "That's what we need to talk about."

Just that quick there was no air in his lungs. No spit in his mouth. "Is she hurt?"

"No." Danny looked uncomfortable, pulling his wrinkled golf shirt down over his gut as he opened the door wider. "Allie's fine."

"A fight?" He'd already started for the office, even though he hadn't entirely processed what the guy meant. Allie took her hockey seriously, and yeah, she was still playing in the coed league at an age when most girls opted for the single-sex, no-contact league, but a fight? A hockey fight? At practice?

That was when he noticed the mess around the skate shop on the opposite side of the lobby. The display in the front window was knocked to pieces, and the glass from the window glinted on the floor. A rack of jackets was overturned near the entrance door. Allie's stick with the distinctive fluorescent purple tape lay partially under the collapsed sandwich board advertising current sales.

He looked back to Danny who tugged at his shirt again.

The top of Allie's head was slightly visible beyond Danny's shoulder in the office. He tried to push by the smaller man but Danny locked his arm, blocking the doorway, and said in a low voice, "I'm sorry about this."

"Let me see her."

Danny stepped back and Bryan was past him and kneeling next to Allie. He barely registered that there were other people in the room as he put his hands on either side of his daughter's chin and raised her head.

Allie. *His girl.* For a second he couldn't focus, he was so relieved that she was in one piece. He stroked her jaw with his thumbs, happy to have her there so close, and then he blinked and her features became clear. Her lip was split, a thin line of blood where the skin was cracked. Her small, upturned nose, with the exact same smattering of freckles his ex-wife had always hated on her own nose, was fine. She had a scratch on one cheek but nothing looked too bad except her eyes. She wouldn't look straight at him, had her gaze fixed somewhere over his shoulder. Allie was scared. Not hurt scared, but scared scared in a way he hadn't seen since those first panicked days three months ago when Erin had told them she was going on tour with Lush and Allie would be staying with him full-time.

What the hell had happened to put that look back in her eyes?

"You okay?" he asked, his voice rough.

When she nodded, he let his eyes skim quickly over the rest of her. There was blood on the neck of the Sabres jersey he'd given her for Christmas and the knee was torn out of her jeans, the skin underneath raw and weeping blood, but she looked all right. She was in one piece and he'd made it home, late but not too late, and whatever else happened, he could handle. He *would* handle. Somehow he'd make this right for Allie because although she deserved the best, all she had right now was him.

He slid one hand around to the back of her neck and then down to rest on her shoulder, reassuring himself as much as her as he turned to stand. His knee protested when he straightened it, but he barely noticed. With his immediate worries answered, the other people in the room finally registered. His gaze jerked from the woman in the chair next to Allie to the boy sitting on the far side. The boy who'd hit Allie. The boy who better have a damn good explanation for himself.

"Danny?" he said, his voice tight. "What happened?"

Danny pointed at the chair and Bryan sat—he had questions, but he trusted Danny to answer them. Danny was a straight shooter. He'd coached Bryan back in squirt hockey, and had never given him bad advice.

Allie's cut knee was jerking up and down a mile a minute next to his. He rubbed her shoulder, trying to release some of her tension but the knee kept bouncing.

"Clare Sampson, meet Bryan James, Allie's father. The kids already know each other," Danny said. "A little too well."

Bryan didn't recognize Clare Sampson. She was dressed more stylishly than most of the hockey moms he saw around the rink; her navy belted car coat couldn't possibly offer much protection from the metal benches. Her straight, sleek brown hair was tucked behind her ears and her eyes were also brown behind a pair of trendy-looking glasses with dark green frames. Her face was attractive, or would have been if she hadn't been glaring at him as though he was a spot on the front of her white silk shirt. She must have kept her own last name because he didn't know any dads named Sampson.

"Allie and Tim got in a pretty serious fight in the skate shop after practice," Danny said. "I was fitting a pair of skates in the back and they were going at it before we could break them up. I haven't taken stock yet, but I'm guessing there's quite a bit of property damage—the front window's broken for sure. Luckily neither of them is hurt too bad."

Bryan leaned forward so he could see around Clare. The boy was sitting slumped in his chair, an ice pack on one eye, the neck of his shirt stretched and the skin underneath scratched. A bruise was blooming on his chin. His good eye was open but as soon as he saw Bryan looking at him, he closed it. Even allowing for the fact that he was a little beat up, Bryan didn't recognize him.

"What happened?" he whispered fiercely to Allie. "How does that kid even know you?"

His daughter's head dipped lower and her knee started bouncing harder so Bryan knew he'd made a mistake even before Clare's mouth tightened and she snapped, "Tim is on the Twin Falls Cowboys, Mr. James. Same as Allie."

Bryan leaned forward again for a second look at the boy and Allie muttered, "Right wing, fourth line."

"Fourth line?" he said. "I didn't think we had a—"

"Dad," Allie said.

At the same instant Tim reopened his good eye and said, "It's only my third week."

"Discussing hockey positions isn't the point," Clare said. "Your daughter started a fight with my son and despite what Mr. Jackson says, Tim is not okay." Bryan was all set to rip into her when she added, "And this is not the first time she's done it."

Not the first time? What did that mean? He looked to Allie, but she was staring at the floor again.

"Mom," Tim protested, his voice cracking.

CLARE KNEW SHE WAS crossing a line her son hadn't wanted her to cross, but she was frankly out of patience.

Allie James was a pretty girl, an excellent athlete and as far as she could see, a hot-tempered bully.

Clare straightened in her chair and patted Tim's arm, but her son jerked away from her, the ice bag he'd been holding on his eye flinging drops of water onto her pants and the linoleum floor. He scuffed the water with the toe of one black sneaker. "I asked you not to do this," he said with an embarrassed glance at Allie.

She ignored the guilt she felt as she said, "What happened, Mr. James, is your daughter attacked Tim after school on at least two occasions and then again tonight. I want to know what you're going to do about that because I'm this close—" Clare held two fingers up, leaving barely a micron of space between them "—to calling the police."

"The police? They're kids."

Despite his dismissive tone, Allie's father sat forward, his attention on her now, not Tim. *Good.* He should know how serious this was and exactly who he was dealing with.

"Ms. Sampson," the manager said. "Let me give Bryan a quick rundown of what happened tonight. I hope we can work this out without getting the police involved."

Clare nodded. She'd give them a few more minutes but if she didn't like what she saw, she was breaking up the boys club and getting some help down here. She might have just moved to Twin Falls while these guys seemed to be old friends, but that didn't mean she had to let them push her or Tim around.

"After practice, Allie and Tim were in the pro shop. Like I said, I was in the back so I didn't see what happened, but Cody MacAvoy was there, and he says Allie jumped Tim."

Clare was watching Allie's father closely. He winced at the manager's last words.

His blue eyes were shadowed by the dark brown hair falling across his forehead. She'd noticed when he came into the office that he was much taller than the rink manager, and that he held himself with confidence despite a slight limp. Now, slumped in the chair next to his daughter, he looked considerably less formidable. He was shooting worried looks at Allie and nodding as the manager told the story, but she wasn't sure how much he was really taking in. If circumstances were different, she could imagine sympathizing with him—this was a horrible situation and the man looked exhausted.

"It took two of us to…uh…pull her off him."

Clare started to reach for Tim, to brush the hair off his forehead at least, to reassure herself, but she saw him tense and so she disguised the gesture by tucking her own hair behind her ear.

She and Tim had always been close—it was just the two of them and had been right from the start.

This year, ever since Tim started seventh grade, he'd been pushing her away. His reach for independence was natural, she knew. Healthy, even. But it scared her.

She'd told him she would stay out of the trouble he'd been having with Allie, but he couldn't expect her to ignore this. She'd been right there in the lobby, half watching a repeat of *Friends* on the TV mounted over the snack-bar window while scrolling through her e-mail in another futile attempt to clear her in-box. Then there'd been yelling and the sound of breaking glass and a horrible cracking sound she figured out later was Tim's head hitting the floor. She'd turned as the kids had come rolling out of the skate shop like some grotesque, many-armed monster. Thank God they'd avoided the broken glass, most of which was off to the side.

She'd never seen a fistfight before and the little she'd witnessed of this one had been brutal and desperate. She'd stood frozen while the rink manager pulled Allie off Tim, and Cody, a boy from their team, helped her son to his feet.

It had taken all of her self-control not to slap Allie's face right there even though she'd never hit another human being in her life. She didn't want to punish Allie for the physical damage she'd caused Tim, but for the anxious, bewildered look on his face as he was helped to his feet. And to be honest, for her own frustration. A thirteen-year-old girl hockey goon was not what they needed now while Tim was trying to get used to a new school and before either of them was comfortable in the new town.

"The kids won't say what started it," the man continued. "In fact, neither of them has said much of anything at all."

Clare put her hands in her lap, squeezing them together hard, letting the discomfort remind herself to be strong here even if it made Tim or Allie or Allie's father unhappy.

"Allie, does Danny have this straight?" Bryan asked.

She lifted her head. "I don't care if she does call the police, I'm not talking about it."

"Allie—"

Clare never found out what Bryan had intended to say because Allie put an end to the conversation by pushing her chair back and running out of the office, slamming the door behind her so hard the pictures rattled on the walls.

Bryan was up and ready to go after his daughter when Clare spoke.

"It's late and we really have to get home if we're going to get any sleep tonight." She heard the frustration in her own voice, unable to care enough to conceal it. "We've accomplished nothing. I don't see any choice but to file a police report, because honestly, Allie's not showing any remorse and I can't believe that Tim is going to be safe here or at school."

Tim slumped lower in his chair, but Bryan looked furious. "I don't know who you are, lady, but you don't know Allie. She's a thirteen-year-old girl, not a monster. You don't call the police over a kids' fistfight."

Clare stood up, refusing to raise her voice, but not willing to back down. "Allie has attacked Tim on three separate occasions. Maybe if she realized that there are consequences for her actions she'd think twice before she does it again."

"You're unbelievable!"

"And you're irresponsible. Your kid is out of control and you don't even know it."

He stared at her, his jaw tight, the blue of his eyes dark under his lowered eyebrows. If she hadn't been defending Tim she might have felt intimidated. Even dressed in what she assumed were his business clothes, there was something about him that suggested strength coiled not too far under the starched dress shirt. He opened his mouth to respond but then made a disgusted sound and turned toward the door. The rink manager grabbed his arm to hold him in the room.

"Clare, I know you have valid concerns," he said. "And, Bryan, I know you want to go after Allie. But I'm hoping instead of lawyers or, God forbid, the police, you'll consider using the mediation program. The offices are right down the block at the community rec center, and I can tell you they get results."

He handed a card to Bryan and stretched across the empty chair to give one to Clare. He looked seriously from her to Tim. "The best thing for the kids is to get them to work this out, not to let it fester. They can start to enjoy themselves on the ice."

Clare felt a spike of anxiety. "Tim's not going back on the ice, not in a hockey uniform. We're finished with hockey."

"Mom," Tim said as he stood up. "I'm not quitting hockey."

He started to brush past her. "Tim, wait," she said.

"I'll be in the car. I'd like you to take me home if you can make the time before you have Allie arrested for giving me a black eye." He dropped the ice bag on the floor and then left the office, slamming the door harder than Allie had. A trophy rocked back and forth and then fell off the bookcase next to the door, but Bryan caught it before it hit the ground.

There was an awkward moment while the three adults stood in the sudden silence. Bryan carefully replaced the trophy, wiping the dust off the base with his finger. Danny broke the tension by saying, "I'm going to have to report this. The board will discuss it. Signing up for mediation will show you're serious about working together and maybe they'll let the kids stay in the league."

"Let them stay?" Bryan said. "Allie's not even supposed to be in this league. She got recruited by the Upstate Select team. If Erin hadn't..." He stopped. "Twin Falls Youth Hockey should be happy to have her."

"The board takes bullying seriously," Danny replied.

"I know." Bryan seemed to lose all his anger as he nodded, rubbing his thumb across the card before slipping it in his pocket as he reached for the door. "I gotta find Allie," he said, looking directly at the rink manager. "If Ms. Sampson wants to pursue this mediation thing, she can get in touch. If not, I guess I'll talk to the police when they come knocking. I'll call you tomorrow about paying for the damage."

He put his hand on the door frame, his knuckles whitening. He took a breath and Clare watched as he consciously relaxed his shoulders. She was sure he'd just counted to ten in his head, and she appreciated that even though he was mad, he was trying to keep his temper in check. If only Allie had some of his self-control. She appreciated even more that this time he made eye contact with her, not his friend.

"Allie's a good kid," he said. "I don't know what went on tonight or the other times, but..." He paused and then repeated quietly, with conviction, "She's a good kid. We've just...it's been a rough year." He gestured toward the ice bag melting on the floor. "I hope your boy is okay."

She wasn't anywhere close to forgiving him or Allie, but she managed a nod. She could acknowledge the effort he'd put into being civil without backing down from her own feelings.

When he was gone, Clare bent to retrieve her purse.

She was drained and all she could think about was going home to crawl into bed with a heating pad and a book. If only all her books weren't still packed in boxes. It didn't really matter, because first she had to decide how to approach this situation and she had to get through to Tim. She wondered what Allie's father would tell his wife, what that would feel like, to share these burdens with another person who loved your child the way you did. Tim spent a month every summer with his dad in Italy, but Matteo had never been involved in Tim's day-to-day life.

The rink manager was watching her. "I'd understand if you called the police," he said quietly. "That fight was scary and they're not even my kids. Still, I've seen the mediation program work wonders. Allie's definitely got problems she should work on. This program might help her."

She was tired of these guys circling the wagons around Allie.

"I'm not sure why you believe I care about Allie's issues," Clare snapped.

"Because her issues are Tim's issues. At least that's how it sounds to me."

"Tim isn't the one hitting people for no reason."

"How do you know there's no reason?"

That stopped Clare. She knew there was no reason because Allie was a bully and Tim was her kid. Her well-adjusted, nonbullying kid. *Right?*

Clare had been sure that Tim hadn't done anything to instigate this trouble. Except now there was a doubt. Not a big one and not something she wanted to consider. But what if Tim were partly responsible? Not that he or anyone ever deserved to get punched. But what if? He'd never been a bully, but he certainly wasn't an angel. He almost always had some behavioral bumps when he was settling into a new school, but his feelings about their latest move were intensely negative.

Obviously she and Tim had some talking to do. The problem was that lately, talking was the one thing they couldn't seem to manage.

CHAPTER TWO

As HE DROVE HOME, BRYAN had half an eye on the road. Allie was silent in the seat next to him, her face flashing in and out of clarity as the shadows thrown by the streetlights blinked across the car. He couldn't really see her. Couldn't tell what was going on with her.

Didn't have any idea what to say.

All he knew was that the kid Clare Sampson described wasn't his kid. His Allie was competitive, driven even, but she wasn't a bully.

Was she?

As soon as that traitorous doubt entered his mind he wanted to step on the gas and drive, take him and Allie down the road to a new town where they could start over. That's what he'd always done, hit the road, let his commitment to his sales job run interference for him. He'd never taken his daughter with him on the road, never expected to have to, because she'd always been safe at home with Erin. He'd understood that his role was to make the money, that was what his wife had wanted from him. But now the roles were changed. He and Erin were divorced last year. Three months ago, she'd left Allie with him, and Allie, apparently, was beating people up left and right.

He hit the blinker before he made the left onto Green Avenue.

Screw Clare and her kid and everyone else. His kid was not a bully. He knew Allie.

What a freaking nightmare.

"Is she really going to call the cops?"

Those were the first words either of them had spoken.

"No. Of course not." He wanted so desperately to reassure her that he lied. He had absolutely no idea what Clare had in mind. What would he want if the situation were reversed; if Tim had been the aggressor? He hoped to hell Clare was a more forgiving person than he was.

He made the last right turn and pulled into their driveway.

"Dad!" Allie said, hunching her shoulders and tucking her face into the front of her Twin Falls Cowboys jacket.

He followed her horrified gaze out the car window to the front of the little white Cape Cod where he and Erin had spent their entire marriage and where Allie and Erin had lived after the divorce.

"Sorry. I forgot." He threw the car into Reverse and pulled out. They'd sold the house when Erin decided to go on the road with the band, and Allie had moved into his apartment. He hadn't had time to keep the house up and Erin wanted the money.

He drove to the apartment complex and pulled into the empty space outside their door. The light over the front door and the one on the deck were both off, the windows dark. The lights were supposed to be on a timer, but it looked as if that was one more system he'd set up that wasn't working the way it was meant to.

"You want to tell me what happened?" he asked.

"Mr. Jackson already did." Allie stared straight ahead

at the dashboard while she spoke. "It was exactly what he said. I punched Tim first and then we had a fight. I…" Her voice wavered and she stopped. When she started again, her tone was more defiant. "I hit him really hard and I wanted to hurt him, but then some grown-ups broke it up and now his mommy is going to call the cops. All right? That's what happened. Exactly that."

Her chest was rising and falling with her rapid breaths.

"Allie, that can't be the whole story."

"It is." she said. A few tears slid down her cheeks. "I beat Tim up and that's it."

Bryan put his hand on her shoulder. "Listen," he started, but she pulled back and opened her door.

"He's an idiot. Why is he even on the team?" she yelled.

"Did he do something or say something to you?"

"No. Nothing."

She slammed the door and ran through the thin coating of snow on the walk. She pulled the extra key out from under the empty planter on the cement steps and opened the front door. He watched it all unfold and he didn't move a muscle.

In his mind, he saw what should happen next. He was supposed to go after her and get this sorted out. If she'd been honest about what prompted the fight, maybe he could have done that. He imagined himself following her into the house. They'd sit at the table in the kitchen and he'd make hot chocolate or they'd share a plate of Oreos. He'd tell her that she was grounded and she'd have to write a letter apologizing to Tim and another one to Danny, and there'd be extra chores so she could work off some of the money for the damages. He'd be stern and she'd be sorry and then he'd make a joke that wasn't very funny and she'd smile anyway and things would be okay again. He'd seen *Full House*. He knew how it was supposed to work.

Except she hadn't been honest. It wasn't as simple as she punched Tim, Tim fell down. He sighed. Thirteen years in sales had taught him about reading people.

He had no doubt that she'd started the fight or that she'd wanted to hurt the kid. She'd definitely told the truth about those parts. But there was more to it than that. She wasn't a bully. She was hurt and angry and something that happened between her and Tim had upset her deeply enough to make her snap.

So yeah. It was his job to reinforce that hitting people wasn't okay. She needed to be disciplined, but she also needed to be helped. Unfortunately for Allie, he'd been caught up in his job for most of her childhood, and even when he'd been around, Erin hadn't let him take the lead on much of the parenting. She'd said it was disruptive to the routine if he did things his way when he was home.

He'd felt so guilty over not being able to give Erin and Allie everything he'd planned that he'd decided the best thing he could do for them was to work and make sure they had everything they wanted. And now that he was in charge he was out of his depth.

He flipped his phone open and scrolled through to Erin's number. She might be off living out her childhood dream of being a hairdresser to the stars, or at least to the latest designer girl band, but she should be able to spare a few minutes to tell him what the hell to do for their daughter. Was it asking too much for him to want some advice? After all, she disrupted the routine in a pretty freaking thorough way when she left them for her job.

Of course, she didn't pick up. She rarely did when he called her. He left a message but didn't go into detail.

He should work out a code with Erin so she'd know which calls she couldn't ignore. He'd text the code word and that would be the sign that he wasn't messing around. The code word could be *Uncle*.

He rested his head on the steering wheel briefly before climbing out and opening the trunk. He grabbed Allie's hockey bag and her stick and his own suitcase and leather laptop case. The skates and gear samples he'd taken on his sales calls could wait until morning.

When he hitched the bags higher on his shoulder, his knee protested, but he refused to baby it. The accident that ended his hockey career had controlled him for a long time, erasing his choices, forcing them to move back to Twin Falls, and him into exactly the kind of sales job his dad had had and that he'd sworn he'd never take. He'd decided years ago that he wouldn't acknowledge the pain from his knee any more than he'd let what might have been rule him.

When he pushed the front door open, the shower was running in the bathroom down the hall. Allie had the music on, too, some band he didn't recognize blasting over the noise of the water, so any chance of an immediate conversation was gone.

Bryan kicked the hockey bag to the side and then unzipped it and took the wet shin guards and socks out. He laid them on the drying rack around the corner in the living room, unrolling the striped blue-and-green socks and shaking out Allie's jersey.

He stretched it flat to dry. Allie's number seventeen

was the same one he'd worn. Same color, same team, same name. James, number seventeen, Twin Falls Youth Hockey.

Erin would have killed him if he'd put the drying rack in the living room when they lived together. Hockey gear smelled like a pungent combination of dampness, sweat and locker room, but to him that smell was home. Before Allie, his best times had been on the ice. Hell, even after Allie, his best times had been at the rink, watching her skate and knowing this was one thing they shared, the one thing he was sure he could talk to her about that he knew better than Erin.

Home hadn't ever been comfortable for him. He'd been out of his parents' house, boarding with strangers during his junior-hockey days by age sixteen. He'd been married before college, and then he and Erin had so much upheaval in the beginning of their marriage. They probably shouldn't have lasted as long as they did, probably wouldn't have if he hadn't been away so much.

Even this apartment, the first place he'd ever lived on his own, felt temporary. He'd picked it because it was close to his old house. Danny and a couple other guys helped him move his stuff in and he'd never done another thing to make it his own. He'd been living there for almost a year before Allie moved in and he'd had to go out and buy silverware and a set of dishes so she didn't have to eat out of take-out containers every night.

He kept planning to get some better furniture or maybe even look for someplace bigger—the apartment had two bedrooms but the living area was small and he and Allie were constantly tripping over each other. He wished he knew what Erin's plans were after the tour ended. She hadn't said she was staying in California, but he didn't really see her coming back to Twin Falls. If she wanted Allie to move to California with her, where would that leave him? Would Allie want to go?

He picked up Allie's stick and leaned it in the corner with the other five or six already balanced against the wall. If only teenage girls were as uncomplicated as a sheet of ice and a couple of nets.

TIM'S ROOM WAS DARK but Clare knocked and when he didn't answer, she went in anyway. He was an indistinct lump under his covers and for a second she was able to fool herself that he was six again and the worst problem in his world was the possibility that Target would be out of the red Power Rangers costume and he'd have to be the blue one for Halloween.

"I'm sleeping," he muttered. Still angry at her.

"Tim, let's talk about this. What are you thinking?"

He sat up abruptly, his face half-lit by the streetlight outside his window. The one eye she could see was swollen almost shut, turning his familiar features grotesque. "What I'm thinking is that you keep butting in when we already talked about Allie and you're supposed to let me handle it."

She came into the room and sat on his bed but he pulled away, lying back down, facing the wall.

"The parameters have changed since I agreed to stay out of this situation."

"I'm not one of your software projects, Mom. You aren't involved. I'm handling it."

"Tim."

"Mom."

"I don't even know what *it* is. Why is Allie bullying you?"

"She's not bullying me."

"I saw what she did to you tonight."

"That wasn't bullying—it was a fight." His tone implied that she was being dense on purpose, but she wasn't. She was trying to understand.

"I don't see the difference if the outcome is you're hurt and she's not."

"Did you want me to hit her back?"

That stopped her. What exactly had she seen? Allie and Tim, rolling on the floor. Had he been defending himself? Was it still bullying if he'd chosen not to fight back? Would she have wanted him to hit the girl?

"Why can't you explain what's going on? Is this your idea of teenage rebellion?"

"Where do you even get this stuff, Mom? It's not rebellion. It's me, living my life. You always want to fix everything for me, but you have to butt out." He pulled the covers tighter over his head. "You can make me move seven times a year, do the new-kid thing every single grade, but you can't tell me how to be me."

Clare sat, taken aback by his anger. She'd seen Tim "do the new-kid thing" as he put it, many times. It hadn't ever bothered him. They moved a lot, following her software security consulting jobs around the country. She'd ridden out the bumpy beginnings often enough to know he'd decided the fastest method to make friends in a new town was to get noticed. Mostly that strategy involved acting up in class or on the school bus. Her son had a lot of energy and when he put his mind to something, he generally saw results. Half the time she'd laughed with him about his efforts to jump-start his social life.

She felt instinctively that this issue between him and Allie was different, more personal and more dangerous.

If only she could be sure she was pushing him to let her help because she was a responsible parent and not because he'd closed her out for the first time.

She jostled the bed as she stood up and Tim twitched the covers even tighter. She didn't lean down and kiss the blanket in the approximate location of his forehead. She didn't smooth the covers across his feet, making sure they were tucked in tight at the bottom of the bed the way he liked. She didn't even touch him gently on the shoulder or give his knee a reassuring pat. The pat would reassure her, but it would make him mad.

She waited for a second.

She knew she had issues. Her only sibling, Gretchen, had been diagnosed with a fatal neuromuscular disease at the age of ten. As soon as they'd gotten the diagnosis for Gretchen, almost before the family had processed the news, the doctors had hustled eight-year-old Clare through testing to find out if she had the same time bomb ticking inside her.

When her tests had come back negative, she'd felt such fierce relief and then horrible guilt. She and Gretchen had always shared everything and suddenly they were on opposite sides of a chasm. For the next ten years, their family had revolved around Gretchen—a desperate search for a cure, treatments meant to slow the inevitable and extend her life, gifts and wish fulfillment and last time to see this, do that, be here, and above all, worry. So many ordinary things—infection, a fall, even overexertion—were dangerous and Clare grew up hemmed in and protected right along with Gretchen. Even emotions were dangerous. How could Clare feel stifled by the caution and care that might be saving Gretchen's life? How could she be angry about anything when she was the one who got to grow up? How could she indulge her wild side when Gretchen was so reduced?

Clare might be overprotective now, but she wasn't an idiot. She knew damn well that the root of her worst, most instinct-driven decisions was buried deep in the screwed-up psyche born of being Gretchen Sampson's healthy little sister.

The trouble was, being aware of her issues wasn't always enough to help her decide if a decision was a good one or one warped by her past.

She backed toward the door, one hand pressed flat against her lips to keep from saying anything that would upset Tim further. It was hard to be silent when her every instinct was screaming at her to help him. *Now.* Her work in computer security was all about immediate action in the face of immediate threats. That world made sense. This wasn't work, though, this was Tim. Immediate wasn't the answer this time.

She flicked on the light in the hall and then pulled his door almost shut. "I love you," she whispered, loud enough for him to hear, soft enough for her to deny he'd heard if he didn't answer her.

"I'm not quitting hockey." His voice was muffled by the blankets. "It's how you fit in here."

It was possible that the only word she hated more than *hacker* was *hockey*.

She pushed the door partway open again. "You're going through a rough time." She understood that much, but she couldn't let him defy her. "That's the only reason I let you stay on the team after you signed up behind my back. If I say you're quitting, you're quitting."

Tim threw off the covers and sat up. "The reason I had to sneak behind your back is because you won't listen to me about what I want. You drag me all over the country for your job and nothing I say matters. If I'd asked you if I could play hockey, what would you have said?"

She took a moment. She wanted to say the right thing but she also wanted to be honest. "I'd have asked why. You were happy figure skating in Baltimore. Why did you want to start hockey now?"

"'Cause," Tim answered, his expression giving her no clues. He pressed on with the relentless teenage antagonism she was still not used to. "Then what would you have said?"

He had her and they both knew it.

"I imagine I would have said no. I have reservations about the risks of hockey, and frankly, Allie is a great example of the kind of kid who plays, the kind of kid I wanted you to avoid."

"That's why I didn't ask." He shook his head and his long hair fell straight across his forehead, making him look younger than he was. "You would have talked me out of it or talked me into something else. Hockey is mine. *I* like hockey. When you live in Twin Falls, you play hockey."

"But the bullying—"

"It's not bullying!" He flopped down and rolled up in his blankets again. "Close the door," he said. "And turn out the light."

Clare nodded. He couldn't see her, but she wanted to acknowledge him, to make it seem as if they were having a conversation, not a shouting match.

She pulled the door shut, turned out the hall light and then went into her own room, fumbling until she found the light switch on the left side of the door when she'd been sure it was on the right. The new house was still unfamiliar. She hoped that would change soon.

When Tim was little, picking up stakes and moving to wherever her next freelance contract led had been exciting. She and Tim would scope out the town, making lists of things they wanted to visit, buying maps, researching on the Internet. They'd both enjoyed discovering a new place, meeting people, trying the local activities. They'd played games memorizing local landmarks so they wouldn't get lost while they learned how to get around.

She hadn't seen Tim's change of heart coming until it was too late. Two years ago when he was in fifth grade, she'd accepted a longer-term contract in Baltimore. The city was terrific and they'd taken full advantage of all the attractions. She'd been having such a good time that she hadn't even really noticed that for the first time, Tim was living somewhere long enough to put down roots. Not just the kind of roots where he knew the pitching rotation for the Orioles, but the kind of roots where he knew his way around his friends' kitchens and got voted class president in sixth grade.

The economy tanked right when her contract was coming to a close and she'd been lucky to get this gig at a local bank in Twin Falls. Relieved to have the work, she probably hadn't paid as much attention as she should have to Tim's protests about having to move again. She'd been so sure his anger was temporary or a general symptom of this personality disorder known as being a teenager.

He wasn't coming around.

He still missed his friends from Baltimore and at the

same time, he was working hard to make sure they also put down roots in Twin Falls. He was digging in.

He'd tried to make her promise they wouldn't move again until after he graduated from high school, but she couldn't. She was on a nine-month contract here. The business economy wasn't anywhere close to stable and, as her recent experience looking for a job had proved, she didn't have a hope of predicting where her next contract would take them.

What a mess.

The house they were renting was bigger than their norm and her bedroom—what the Realtor had called a master suite—stretched the entire southern wall of the house. There were built-in bookcases on either side of the door. She'd brought two cartons of books up from the garage before she left for the rink, but she didn't have the energy or the interest to unpack them now. She lifted one box onto the other and slid the stack back against the wall.

Standing at the foot of the bed, she started to undress, putting her blouse in the net bag she used to store her dry cleaning, wiping her shoes with the soft cloth she kept in her closet before sliding them into the shoe bag, choosing a set of blue-and-white striped pajamas. She picked her coat up from the end of the bed and put it on a hanger, but then reached into the pocket and pulled out the card the rink manager had given her. What was his name? Jackson. Bryan had called him Danny. She would have to remember that.

The card read "Community Mediator, Lila Sykes." Followed by a phone number and the line, "No one should have to do this alone."

True, Clare thought. She might be alone in this new

town, but that didn't mean she had no one to talk to. Her computer was on the desk near the window. She sat down and called up a video-phone screen for Lindsey, her best friend. The time difference from New York to Seattle meant it was early enough that Lindsey might be out at dinner, but luckily, she was home. Seeing her, so familiar, so dear, almost made Clare start crying.

"Hey!" Lindsey said. "I've been dying for a distraction, how did you know?"

"I wish I could say I'm psychic, but the truth is, I need advice."

"Shoot."

"Tim got in another fight with that girl I was telling you about. A bad one this time."

"Is he okay?" Lindsey was Tim's godmother and his number-one fan.

"Fine. I don't know how, but he's fine."

"For God's sake, Clare, what is wrong with that girl? Where are her parents?"

"I met her dad tonight. He…well…let's just say he doesn't seem to know his daughter very well."

Lindsey held her fists up to shadow box the screen. "Say the word and I'll come out there and teach him and his spawn some respect."

"We've had enough punching around here."

"I could egg his car, at least."

Clare smiled for the first time in what felt like forever. Lindsey was so much more to her than a friend. They'd met the first day of kindergarten and—except for a three-month stretch in seventh grade when they'd stopped talking while they both tried to attract Gene Fisk, the first boy in their grade to hit six feet—they'd been best friends ever since. Lindsey had idolized

Gretchen every bit as much as Clare had and she'd been the only one of all their friends who'd really understood what it felt like when she'd died.

Lindsey's house had been Clare's refuge. With four kids in the family and a rotating lineup of pets, the house had been chaotic enough that Clare was forced to be outgoing when she was there. She could finally relax and be herself.

She and Lindsey had gone to Stanford together and now her friend worked as a software test engineer in Seattle. Lindsey's house was down the street from the one she'd grown up in, where her parents still lived. She was Clare's emergency contact, the executor of her will and the only person who'd been at every single one of Tim's birthday parties. After Clare's mom died and her dad continued to grow more distant, Lindsey's steadfast friendship had come to mean more to her every year.

Clare's face felt hot and there were tears in her eyes. She hadn't realized how much she wanted to talk to Lindsey about Tim's attitude.

"How about instead you tell me what to do next?" She pushed her glasses up on her forehead to rub her eyes. "He's really mad at me about moving him again. I understand what he's saying, that we don't live the same way as other people. But that's always been okay with him. We get to see all these new places and meet people and we're not tied down. Do you think he actually wants to settle down or could this be a phase or...I don't know...him pushing back against me and my values?" She was talking too fast.

"Your values?" Lindsey asked. "You move all the time because of your values?"

Clare was confused by Lindsey's surprise. "What does that mean?"

"Nothing. I guess I never realized. I'm sorry," Lindsey said. "What I mean is I assumed you were eventually going to land somewhere, once you got to the point where you could…" Lindsey shrugged on the computer screen.

"Could what?" Clare asked.

"Relax?" Lindsey suggested.

"What does that even mean?"

"It means, for a while there, your life was a minefield. In the space of four years Gretchen died, you had Tim, you graduated from college and then your mom died. I didn't blame you for wanting to get far away from Seattle. It made sense that you weren't ready to really connect with anyone or build new relationships."

"Freelancing meant I had more time for Tim," Clare said.

"It's been good for you." Lindsey put one finger on the screen. "Listen, I'm not trying to fight. It's just, I guess because you never sold the house here that I always thought you'd be back."

"I can't sell it, Lindsey, but I can't come back."

Clare's mom had died in a car accident while driving home alone at night from a bereavement support group. Her father moved into an apartment a few years later and gave Clare the house. Tim had been about two at the time and she had briefly considered settling in Seattle, close to Lindsey and her father, but she hadn't been able to face living in the house. Frankly, she thought her dad gave it to her because he couldn't stand to live there or to sell it, either. Her dad was more and more withdrawn, even from Tim, so she could only guess at his feelings.

She tried not to think about the place beyond making sure the taxes were paid and that when she signed with new renters they had decent references.

"I worry about you sometimes," Lindsey said. "You have so much to offer if you ever decide to put down roots somewhere. Maybe Seattle isn't that place, but maybe there is a place that could be home for you." She paused. "If you're ready for a home. Which you might not be."

"Maybe for me, home isn't one place, it's a feeling. How I feel about Tim and you. Can't that be true?"

Lindsey shrugged. "It can be. But is it? For Tim, too?"

Clare looked out the window into the dark backyard. A spotlight mounted on the house lit the snow-covered bushes. "If my son was going to lobby for a permanent address, I don't know why he picked this one. It's freezing cold and all anyone wants to talk about is hockey. I mean, we lived in Monterey, we were in Baltimore, we had that place with the river in the backyard in Indiana...and he's digging his heels in over Twin Falls, New York?"

"It might not be where so much as when. He's thirteen. I bet being the new kid is harder in middle school."

"That's what he said."

"I'm not colluding with him, I swear, but I remember how tough middle school was, and it got worse every year straight through high school. Maybe he's nervous about fitting in."

"He doesn't seem nervous. He seems mad." Clare sighed. "What's with all the maybes, anyway? You're supposed to be telling me what to do."

Lindsey frowned. "I should probably skip the advice

and just come throw eggs. I bet I'm better at revenge than I am at sympathy."

"If I decide vandalism is the appropriate response, you're my first choice for second-in-command."

"Throwing eggs is hardly ever appropriate, Clare," Lindsey said in a prim tone. "I believe the phrase you're looking for is 'emotionally satisfying.'"

"Thanks, Lindsey. I'm pleased I picked an appropriately bloodthirsty godmother for Tim."

"I got your back, my friend. Fists or eggs, whatever you need."

LATER, AS SHE LAY ON her side, holding the extra pillow close to her chest, listening to another snowstorm tapping on her window, the fight played over and over in her mind. With everything she did to keep him safe, that mess had happened right under her nose. She heard the crack of Tim's head on the ground, the shattering of the window, him saying, "I'm handling it."

Tim didn't understand yet that so much about life couldn't be handled. You could go along the way her parents had with your two daughters and your ordinary life on a friendly street in a good neighborhood and life could still run so far off the rails you'd never find your way back.

No one could expect to handle life. Loving anyone sometimes seemed like the biggest, stupidest mistake you could make. She couldn't un-love Lindsey or her dad, and Tim was a part of her own soul, but she could try her best to keep him safe.

That must be what all parents wanted, right?

She remembered the confusion and determination in Bryan James's voice when he'd told her that Allie was a good kid. She wondered what he'd said to Allie once he caught up with her. Did he have the right answers? Or was his house full of the kind of empty upset that hers was?

CHAPTER THREE

BRYAN TRIED TO TALK to Allie over breakfast but she studied her bowl of Frosted Mini-Wheats cereal with complete concentration and refused to answer his questions. He followed her down the hall when she went to the shower but stopped when she closed the bathroom door in his face. He knocked.

"I'm getting ready for school, Dad."

Not that long ago, "getting ready for school" meant scrambling into her boots and snowpants before she ran to the bus. Now it meant an hour in the bathroom doing God knew what. Actually, Erin would have known what she was doing. Would have been able to help her with it. He hated feeling so useless.

"I can't pretend nothing happened, Allie."

She turned the shower on.

He spun around, but there wasn't anything handy for him to kick. She was so good at avoiding him, but that was how they'd gotten into this mess. He didn't know what was going on with her and based on what Clare had said, he'd already missed a lot. The trouble was, she wasn't going to talk to him about it. Not voluntarily, anyway.

She stayed in the bathroom until about forty-five seconds before the bus pulled up out front. He'd retreated to the kitchen, leaving the hallway empty, letting her think she had a clear shot at escape. When she got to the entryway, he waylaid her, positioning himself between her and the door as she stepped into her sneakers, shrugged on her backpack and flipped her braid over her shoulder. Even though he was squarely blocking the door, she did an excellent job of pretending she was alone, not even glancing at him when she accidentally stepped on his foot.

"You're grounded," he said abruptly. "Come home straight after school."

Finally she looked up, her mouth open. "Grounded until when?"

"Until you sit down and tell me what's going on."

She closed her mouth. He prayed he wouldn't cave. The bus beeped. He willed her out the door. She didn't move. The bus door groaned as it closed and she flicked a glance over his shoulder to the road.

"Fine," she said. "Fine. It's not like I have anywhere to go, anyway."

The bus beeped again. The driver wouldn't wait much longer.

"Can I go to school, or am I grounded from that, too?"

He stepped aside and she pushed the door open. Snow swirled in around their feet. The storm door closed behind her with a snap, cutting the cold air off.

He stood watching her, but the glass fogged as she climbed onto the bus and he lost track of her. "Have a good day," he said, knowing it was inane but wishing there was some way she could hear him.

He slammed the inside door closed and smacked it with his palm.

You're grounded? He'd never grounded anyone before. Where had that come from?

In the kitchen, his cell phone lay next to his laptop on the table. He called Erin. Screw her if it was only 5:00 in the morning in L.A. Her fault for moving so damn far away from her kid.

She didn't answer, and he left a short message to call him. She probably wouldn't. It usually took about three tries before he could contact her and it was a rare day when she actually called him back anytime during daylight hours.

She was busy, she'd say.

Bryan picked up Allie's bowl and took it to the dishwasher. He put the box of cereal back in the cupboard and wiped off the table. Erin was busy all right.

Busy leading her new life. The divorce last year hadn't exactly been a surprise. They hadn't been close since before Allie went to kindergarten. When they slept together it had been about physical release, not love. But she'd been a good mom to Allie. They hadn't been girlfriends like some of the moms and kids he saw on TV, but their relationship was decent. He thought it was, anyway. Who could tell, though?

During the course of their divorce, he'd learned exactly how much Erin had hidden from him. She'd had an affair with some guy she met at karaoke night at the Holiday Inn. She'd claimed she was restless, but the affair hadn't satisfied her any more than being married to him had.

So she'd given up men and started taking classes and entering hairstyling competitions. She'd flown out to Los Angeles for a weeklong workshop and shortly after she got back she'd filed for divorce.

He hadn't fought her on custody because it had never occurred to him that she would want to leave Twin Falls. It made sense that he'd get an apartment, he'd keep his travel schedule and he'd see Allie on the weekends.

He'd had no idea Erin was looking for more than a release from him until she'd blindsided him and Allie again at the beginning of the summer. She tried out for and was cast on a reality show following the U.S. tour of the girl band Lush. The show hired stylists and a hair-and-makeup crew to travel with the band for six months.

When Erin left on the tour in September, he'd cut a deal with his boss to scale back his traveling, and arranged for his sister to watch Allie when he was away. But he'd been pitifully unprepared to face their new reality. He used to have two jobs: earn the money and deal with Allie's hockey. Since Erin left them, he'd encountered a whole world of unfamiliar challenges—and even the two things he'd always done well were messed up. His sales numbers were off and with this fight, Allie was in danger of losing hockey. He'd never expected to be a single dad and now, all signs indicated he was screwing it up.

Bryan picked up the dishcloth and wet it, running the water hot and then wringing the cloth out. He wiped the table, lifting the place mat from Allie's place and then his, and shifting the stack of school papers she'd unloaded from her backpack.

Her grades were slipping. There was a science test buried in the stack with a red note on the top that read, "See me." He wondered if Allie had followed through. Should he call the teacher and find out?

He turned the test over and glanced at the questions,

but then dropped it back on the table and shifted a pile of other papers on top of it. He backed up a step. Nothing, not the night he wrecked his knee, not losing his scholarship, not even the day he'd crawled to Danny for a job after he flunked out of college, had knocked him on his butt as hard as failing Allie.

"Damn it, Erin." He banged his fist on the table and then threw the dishcloth at the sink. It landed with a splat and slid down to settle in a cereal bowl half-full of water. He hated feeling incompetent.

Bryan turned his back on the kitchen, grabbed his keys and his skate bag, and headed for the rink. The locker room was empty when he got there. He sat on the uneven green bench and carefully buckled his knee brace over his jeans before strapping on his skates.

Fifteen minutes after he pulled into the lot, he was on the ice. He pushed himself hard, ignoring the protests from his knee, as he powered through lap after lap.

He was the only one skating. Danny had open-ice times most mornings but other than a moms-and-toddlers group that came on Thursday mornings, not many people got out here on weekdays. He was glad to be alone. Glad he didn't have to see anyone and could let the ice and the speed and the cold air fill his mind with nothing but white and the rhythmic pattern of red and blue lines rushing under his skates.

This was what he knew how to do. He didn't have to think, his muscles were trained and his body did the work. At the center line, he forced a full stop, spraying ice off his blades. Pushing off in the opposite direction, he savored the pull in his muscles when he dug deep on the crossovers.

He'd almost been one of the lucky ones, the guys

who got to make a living playing sports. He could have put his body to work for Erin and Allie. Instead, he'd thrown that chance away on a drunken stunt.

He understood now that getting drafted, getting his scholarship, hadn't meant much. They were merely steps on the long road to the NHL, but at the time, he and Erin both felt he'd gotten his ticket. They hadn't counted on him wrecking his knee at the end of his sophomore season. After the surgeries, he'd worked at his rehab harder than he'd ever worked at anything, but the knee never came back to what it was and his future in the NHL was gone before he'd even had a taste.

It didn't take him long to flunk out of school, losing his chance at a degree and a job with a future.

He and Erin wound up living in Twin Falls in the apartment over his sister's garage. Erin rented a chair in a local salon and got pregnant a few weeks later. Danny gave him a reference and he got a small territory as a sales rep for Dutton Skates, a company that made hockey equipment and team gear, which he'd gradually expanded until he was making a decent living and they'd been able to buy their own house. He'd tried to make it enough, but the weight of disappointments and regret had crushed their family, he thought, almost from the start.

Bryan pushed harder, trying to get himself to the place where he could stop worrying and just be. The ice swept under him, the boards flashed past. But every time he almost got himself to the zone, he'd see Allie the way she'd looked last night in the car. Defeated. Alone. Scared.

He pulled up short again, giving his knee another excuse to complain, and bent over, gripping his thighs, trying to catch his breath and wondering if he'd ever be able to breathe right again.

Someone banged on the glass and he looked over his shoulder. *Danny.* He kept his head down for another minute until he was sure he had himself under control and then skated to the door and let himself out.

"Figured you'd be here," Danny said. "How's Allie?"

Bryan shrugged. "How would you be if you were her?"

"Did Clare call Lila Sykes?"

Bryan pushed the sleeves back on his fleece. "Who's Lila Sykes?"

"She's the mediator, Bry." Danny frowned.

"I haven't heard from anyone yet."

"Well, if you haven't heard from the police, maybe that means she's not going that route."

Bryan should be grateful, but he wasn't. Clare was scared, he got that. Heck, he was scared, too, and with more reason since by all accounts it was Allie who was running wild. But knowing what Clare might be dealing with didn't make him feel any more charitable toward her.

"I almost wish she had called the police. Can you imagine a cop actually filling out a report for a kids' fistfight?"

He expected Danny to agree with him, but the other man responded quietly, "You weren't there."

"What's that supposed to mean?"

"It means—" Danny stopped. He tucked his shirt in nervously. He wasn't going to say whatever he'd started with. "It just means Allie could stand to talk to someone.

She's been through a lot and she seems…angry. Not the Allie I'm used to."

"But won't forcing them together drag it out? Why is it a good idea to make her spend time with the kid she's got a beef with?"

"Because they would get the beef resolved. She could start to move on."

Move on from whatever was bugging her about Tim or from all the other stuff that had to be bugging her? Bryan didn't want to get into any of that.

"Who is that Tim kid, anyway?" he asked. "I never saw him around."

"They moved here right before the season started." Danny's phone rang and he looked at the screen. "Wait one sec. It's John Langenforth."

Bryan rocked back on the heel of his right skate, trying to stretch some of the tightness out of the muscles around his knee. He shouldn't have pushed it that hard.

Danny gave him a thumbs-up as he ended the call. "John's trying to set up a meeting for you and Tim's mom."

"Only the mom?" Bryan asked.

"I haven't seen a dad."

"Is she divorced? What's the kid's sign-up sheet say?"

Danny bent and tugged at a worn piece of sealant on one of the rubber floor tiles. "That's confidential. I can't discuss it with someone who's not on the league board."

"Quit trying to recruit me for the board."

"You know damn well I'm really trying to recruit you to coach."

When a client wanted to cancel an order or make a return after the contract date and Bryan had no intention of either pissing the client off or letting them go, he had a special voice he used. It was equal parts empathy and firmness. *I hear you, but you're out of luck.* He tried it on Danny. "I understand the shortage of qualified coaches, but I don't have the time to take on an additional responsibility."

"Bullshit," Danny said. "Don't give me that salesman crap. You never miss her games. You could work it out—get a decent assistant coach and you'd be all set."

He couldn't believe Danny was bugging him about coaching. It was so obvious he was doing a bang-up job as a dad, why not give him another dozen or so kids he could mold and shape? He could squeeze the disciplinary hearings with the board in around practice.

"I had the pleasure of playing for my dad, Danny. I'm not going to inflict that on Allie."

"You're not your father," Danny said. "And Allie's not you."

"Forget it. She loves playing. I'm not bringing any of that James Family professional hockey crap out there and polluting her game."

He connected with Allie over hockey and at this point in their lives, that was it. He wasn't going to risk messing that up.

"You seriously think you'd ruin the fun for her? You'd be a good coach precisely because you know how wrong it can turn out."

"It's not going to happen," Bryan said, hoping to end the conversation. "What's the mom's name again?"

"Clare," Danny said. "Clare Sampson. She does something with computers."

That seemed to fit with the little he'd seen of her. Last night she'd been controlled, maybe cold. No...not cold. Tough. She'd been ready to take him on, her pointed chin and sleek hair contrasting with big brown eyes she hid behind those smart-lady glasses.

"She wasn't backing down last night, was she?"

"She doesn't seem like the backing-down type."

Would she be willing to meet him? His pulse kicked up again almost as hard as it had been going when he was on the ice. What the hell? He recognized the feeling—the anticipation of looking forward to seeing a hot woman—but he hadn't felt this way in years.

He shouldn't be feeling that way now because there was no way he thought Clare was hot. Haughty, more likely. Aloof. Convinced his kid was some kind of thug. Nowhere in that package was there room for anticipation.

Except he'd really liked the way her hair shone, so perfectly smooth and silky where it swept her neck. And there'd been something about how she looked at Tim that made him imagine if she might know what he was talking about if he shared his worries about Allie.

The glass doors from the lobby opened and John Langenforth walked in.

"Bryan," he said. "Danny."

Bryan had grown up with John. He'd been the instigator of more locker room shenanigans than any two kids combined, and was still the only player in the history of the Twin Falls League to draw a penalty for mooning a ref while the puck was in play. After college, he'd come home and worked himself up to afternoon deejay for the local classic-rock station. John was also the president of the Twin Falls Youth Hockey board.

Three minutes ago, Bryan would have taken an oath that John was incapable of being serious. Judging by the expression on the other man's face now, he'd have been wrong.

John unzipped his Twin Falls Hockey parka. "I guess you know why I'm looking for you."

Bryan nodded.

"I'm sorry we're in the middle of this mess, Bryan. But now that the fight's been reported, the board has to address it. The national organization has a bullying policy and we could lose our standing. I want you to know we'll do everything we can to help Allie."

Bryan nodded, more than uncomfortable with his friend's implication. "I understand."

And he did, too well. John's son was on Allie's team and he wasn't the only parent counting on her to get the team to the state tournament. He still remembered John's delight when he found out Allie wouldn't be able to play on the select travel team this season. The supposedly blind draft had somehow landed Allie on a team with John's kid and the sons of two other board members.

Antibullying policy or not, there was little chance John was going to drop Allie from the roster. This kind of blatant favoritism was one of the reasons Bryan had wanted her on the select team in the first place. She'd have been one of the better kids on that team, but she wouldn't have been the big fish she was in the Twin Falls pond. He couldn't have her cultivating unrealistic ideas about her talent. That was what led him straight to the end of his playing days.

"Danny told me he suggested mediation and the board talked it over this morning. We agreed that if Allie and Tim complete mediation, she can stay on the team."

John wasn't able to meet his eye when he added, "If they don't go for the mediation, we'll have no choice but to deactivate Allie's membership in the league."

Kick her out was what he meant. John couldn't bring himself to say the words so clearly, but that was what he meant.

"But no reason to consider that," John said. "Allie will manage this if she has to, right?"

Suddenly, he couldn't take them looking at him.

"Call me when you have the meeting set. I'll be there." He made a show of checking the scoreboard clock. "I have to head out. Appointments."

John cleared his throat. "Actually, Tim's mom is on her way here. Danny told me you were on the ice so when she said she had time, I figured we might as well lock it down. We can reschedule if we have to, but Allie can't practice until this is settled."

Bryan looked out the doors toward the lobby. Of course Clare wasn't here yet. She couldn't have gotten here so fast.

He wished he'd had time to plan what to say, but maybe this was better. Clare was brand-new territory for him. He could keep lying to himself or he could admit that he found her attractive. She was different from the other women he knew, self-contained and a little fierce. With the divorce finally sinking in those instincts he'd buried for so long were waking up again. It didn't matter why he was attracted. He had to ignore it, end of story.

The important point was that Allie could play hockey if Clare went along with mediation. Persuasion was familiar ground at least; he was more than used to sales. Needing her cooperation and wanting her complicated the situation. Next time Allie decided to pick on someone, he certainly hoped the kid's mom wasn't cute.

"I'll go change." He lifted his hand, nodded at the other two and turned away. He felt their eyes on him as he walked around the edge of the ice to the locker room door. He'd come to the rink to leave his frustrations on the ice and instead everything and everyone had come crowding in with him.

He unbuckled his knee brace and let it slide to the floor while he rested against the cinder-block wall behind him. Digging in his pocket, he pulled out his cell phone. He typed in Allie's number. She'd been the one who taught him to text, laughing at the typos his big fingers made on the tiny keypad.

"You okay?" he typed and then pressed Send. She wasn't supposed to text in class, wasn't even supposed to have her phone on, so there was a good chance she wouldn't answer even if she wanted to. He set the phone next to his gloves on the bench. He waited but it sat silent.

If Allie texted him back before he got his skates off, he decided, that was the sign that Clare was going to be reasonable. He bent and untied the knot on his right skate. He didn't dawdle, it wasn't fair to try to manipulate a sign, but he couldn't help noticing moisture on the skate blade which meant an extra careful wipe dry before he stowed the skate in his bag. He'd just tugged the lace out of the top set of holes on his left skate when the phone buzzed. He grabbed it, flipping the screen open. She'd texted back, "OK."

He dropped the phone on the bench and tugged his skate off quickly. *OK*. He snorted. The two of them didn't have a single conversational skill to split between them. Still, short and unsatisfying as OK was, she'd replied. He zipped his bag and wished he still believed in luck.

CHAPTER FOUR

THE HOCKEY LEAGUE BOARD must have been up before dawn, Clare thought, if they'd had time to meet and still call her before Tim left for school. Fanatics were always so…fanatical.

She'd agreed to meet mostly just to get off the phone because she'd wanted to talk to Tim. But before she had a chance, he'd shouted that he was leaving and slammed the front door. She called his cell. When he answered, he said it was too cold to talk while he was walking.

She took a quick shower and then was lucky enough to get Lila Sykes, the mediator, on the phone, but that conversation hadn't gone well, either. Lila had homed in on the fact that they moved a lot and most of her suggestions were aimed at making Tim feel at home in Twin Falls. Every time she said "settle" or "connect," Clare felt more sure mediation was the wrong move for them at this time. Sure, she wanted Tim to enjoy himself while he was here, but they weren't staying and there was no sense getting involved in a program that would make it harder to leave when her contract redesigning the data security for the Twin Falls Savings bank was up.

The hockey league would have to find another solution for Allie.

When Clare got to the rink, Danny Jackson and John Langenforth, the man she'd spoken to on the phone, met her in the same cluttered office off the lobby where she'd waited for Bryan the night before. They told her Bryan would be here soon and then excused themselves because there was an issue with the bylaws they should discuss in private.

She put her leather backpack down next to a chair, but she didn't sit. She was chilly and nervous, on edge about this discussion and about Tim, and unhappy being in this room again.

The office was cold—probably people who spent their lives inside a hockey rink didn't feel cold the way normal people did. Or maybe it was growing up in Twin Falls that made them impervious to cold. It was only November and already she'd forgotten that she even had toes, let alone what they felt like.

All signs of the confrontation last night were gone. All that was left, according to John Langenforth, was for her to agree to mediation and the entire incident would be swept away. Except the part where she didn't trust Allie and didn't want Tim playing hockey. And the part where she didn't want any hand in mediation. And the part where she was worried about her family. Tim was pulling away so fast. Wishing for things she had no idea how to provide. She wasn't even sure she knew what he wanted when he asked to stay in one place. Did he know?

Was it simply this?

A spot on this hockey team? Maybe the chance to belong to a place so the seasons became yours and you wouldn't notice cold that would shock an outsider?

The walls of Danny's office were covered with framed photos of kids and teams, and the desk was a clutter of files and magazines with sticky notes. Clare bet it would take her less than five minutes to find his online bank account and voice-mail passwords on those notes. After ten years in the computer security field, she never failed to be amazed at the cavalier attitude people took toward their private information. His password was probably *hockey* or *puck*. Men liked their passwords easy to type.

The door to the office opened, startling her away from the desk.

"Sorry," Bryan said. "I thought Danny and John were in here."

He had a hockey bag slung over his shoulder and a blue stick gripped in his right hand. He dropped the bag on the floor near the door, the chest and shoulder muscles under his shirt moving with tantalizing strength. His dark hair was damp, swept back from his forehead with little wings curling out around his ears and at the back of his collar. He must have just come from the shower; she caught a faint hint of soap and spicy aftershave.

He was wearing a navy crewneck sweater with a white T-shirt underneath and soft gray corduroys. When he straightened up, she was struck by how tall he was. She'd noticed the difference between him and Danny last night, but even on his own he was tall, and with his broad shoulders and the muscle she'd seen in his chest, he was...oh no. *No.*

Her body was not going to react to him. He was gorgeous and built, and in this tiny office with her he seemed to be breathing all the available air, but she was here for Tim, not chasing some guy. Bryan James was a parent, not a man.

She swallowed and tried to think about anything besides what it would feel like to tangle her fingers in the hair at the base of his neck.

"They stepped out to look at the bylaws," she said. "They should be back any minute."

He nodded, his mouth tight. Was he angry? Nervous? As confused about his kid as she was?

He sat in the same chair he'd been in last night and she stayed where she was near the wall of photos. Snow slid off the roof overhead with a crunching grind and they both glanced up, but neither of them said anything.

The silence stretched.

Working as a consultant meant she joined existing companies or groups, recommended changes and facilitated shifts in products and systems. Most of the time, she came on the scene after a breach of data security when the company was already out time, money and reputation. She was used to being around people who were on edge and uncomfortable around her. She was also used to not caring how those people felt about her as long as they managed to work logically on the issues. She'd never experienced quite this level of strained silence before.

A small voice in her head murmured that maybe she was uncomfortable because Bryan was attractive, male and just plain took up space in a way most guys, especially the tech guys she was used to, couldn't.

She cleared her throat and watched him, hoping he'd pick up on her signal that he should start talking.

It was bad enough she was going to be the only woman in this meeting with three old hockey pals, she didn't care to fall into the traditional female role of small-talk facilitator.

Nothing.

He seemed perfectly capable of sustaining an uncomfortable silence for hours. Gender roles be damned, she was ready to break the silence herself, except how? *Hey, Bryan, did you figure out why your child hates my child yet?*

Where the hell was his wife? Weren't meetings about the kids like this traditionally the wife's job? Shouldn't Allie's mother at least have come with him? She thought she'd seen a woman driving the car when Allie got dropped off at practice last night. So where was she this morning? The tension might have been eased if there were another person here. Certainly she would find it easier not to fantasize about the man's hair if his wife were sitting next to him.

Would his wife have made time for this if they were meeting at the police station instead of the hockey rink?

Enough.

Not only was she developing a case of baseless animosity toward the missing Mrs. James, she was dangerously close to being affronted on Bryan's behalf.

"Your wife couldn't make it this morning?" she asked.

"No," he said.

Well, that had been spectacularly unsuccessful as far as conversation starters went. He hadn't looked at her, was sitting with his chin down, studying his hands, a worried wrinkle between his eyebrows.

"Is she working?" Clare tried again. *So much for getting away from the topic of his wife.* Why was her brain so uncooperative?

"Sleeping probably. She's in California." He twisted the silver ring he wore on his right hand. She realized then he didn't have a ring on his left. Even before he continued, she started to recalculate.

If he wasn't married…she sneaked a glance at his hair and then linked her hands behind her back. He was cute, but he was a dad whose daughter was bullying Tim. He wasn't a man. Not to her.

"Actually," Bryan said, "she's on the road with Lush. The girl band? They have that song, 'Little Me'?" He looked at her as if she might recognize the name but she didn't. "Anyway, I never know exactly where she is. I can't keep the schedule straight."

"She's in a band?" Clare was shocked enough to forget about his hair and her fingers. Bryan was over thirty, she was sure of it. How old was his wife? "I thought I saw a woman dropping Allie off."

"Must have been my sister. She watches her when I'm out of town. My…Allie's mom is on the crew. She does the hair." He twirled his hand in the air near his ear as if his wife liked to create Princess Leia style ear buns for the band. He sounded angry. He paused and then asked, "Where's Tim's dad?"

Clare felt her cheeks heat up. She was sure the aggression in his tone was payback for her prying. She supposed she deserved it because she had been poking into his business, but the man couldn't expect that he'd say his wife was on the road with a band and people wouldn't want to know more.

"Tim's dad lives in Italy. We don't see much of him."

Bryan studied her for a moment and she wondered how much emotion he could see in her face.

"Well," Bryan finally said. "I guess it's just the two of us then." He crossed his arms on his chest, which did amazing things to his shoulders under the fine knit of his sweater. The combination of hard muscle and soft fabric was making her hands twitch again.

She turned her back to study the photos on the wall. She realized that, of course, the one right in front of her was Bryan. His name was printed on a piece of tape on the bottom of the picture. Once she knew it was him, she recognized the man in the boy.

He was about ten and he was facing the camera, hefting a trophy that looked as if it was made out of a traffic cone spray-painted gold. A bunch of grinning boys surrounded him with their fingers in the number-one sign, all of them soaked in sweat with their hair sticking up and ice caked on their hockey socks. Bryan was head and shoulders taller than most of the kids and he looked...well...he looked exactly how a ten-year-old hockey champion should. Cocky. Thrilled. Adorable.

Why couldn't he have been a thug?

She scanned the wall and discovered there were quite a few photos of him at different ages. In most of them he was holding awards or trophies. Perfect. Tim had tangled with the daughter of Twin Falls hockey royalty.

She spotted a more formal one, from when he was in his late teens, probably his college team. His smile was just as cocky as it was in the first picture she'd seen, but this older version seemed to include not only joy, but a promise. A sinful promise. She wondered how many girls had fallen for his smile back then.

He hadn't uncrossed his arms, but he was looking at her, must have been watching her. His eyes were so guarded, so different from the boy in the photos behind her. Had she hurt him by asking about what seemed to be a difficult family situation?

"I didn't mean to pry about your wife," she said. "I was trying to find something to say and that came out."

"At least you didn't ask who I voted for." He sighed. "Forget it. I still wonder where she is half the time. But to be clear, she's my ex." He held up his ring-free left hand.

Clare nodded and held up her bare left hand. "I never had one in the first place."

He started to smile but then stood up abruptly, the motion bringing him near her, startling her with his sudden closeness and the way the room seemed even smaller. The spots of color high on his cheekbones, probably from the heat of his recent shower, deepened. She stood her ground, looking up to him, and for a second neither of them moved. Then he spun, pacing the few feet toward the far wall, away from her.

"Listen, Clare. My kid is in big trouble because you accused her of bullying your son. I don't intend to sit here and swap life stories." He crossed his arms on his chest again. "No offense."

Clare let out an impatient breath. *No offense, my ass.*

"I thought we were here to talk about mediation. Shouldn't we set a good example?"

"I'm not planning to bully you," Bryan said slowly and deliberately. "So as long as you're not planning to bully me, I'd say we're good."

HE SHOULDN'T HAVE SAID that, Bryan conceded. He'd meant to keep quiet until Danny and John came back. Instead he sure had ticked Clare off. She had a wide mouth, with corners that turned up naturally, making her always seem as if she was on the verge of smiling.

Except she wasn't smiling at him after that remark. Her mouth had tightened to a thin line.

He was just so sick of people making him feel as though he didn't know what he was doing. He was perfectly capable of making himself feel incompetent. And if he needed any reinforcement, he had his sister who'd chewed him out for being late to get Allie, at least half of Allie's teachers who were concerned about her attitude and a whole mess of other people who never seemed to miss an opportunity to mention how Erin liked to run things.

"Are you *serious?*" Clare asked, her brown eyes flashing. He'd noticed the night before that her pronunciation got sharper when she got mad, as if she were biting each word off individually.

"What did you expect?" he said.

"I expected that we'd meet here and try to work out this problem like civilized people."

"Was that a crack about Allie?"

"What?"

"*Civilized?* She lost her temper. That doesn't mean she's not civilized."

"Lost her temper?" Clare took a step toward him. "She slammed Tim's head off the floor!"

"Well, since she hasn't hit anybody else, I'm curious what Tim did to make her hit him."

"What he did—"

The door opened and John and Danny came back into the office. "We're ready," John said. Danny looked worried as he glanced between them.

Clare's mouth snapped shut. Bryan forced himself to lean back against the wall. *God.* He couldn't believe they'd been shouting at each other. He hated that Clare saw Allie as a punk. He wanted to make her understand how wrong she was, but instead he kept making things worse.

John held up a stack of stapled paper. "We went over the league bylaws and the solution is legal. So, if the kids go to mediation and successfully complete the course, everything is settled. Allie keeps her spot on the team and we relax and enjoy the ride while the Twin Falls Cowboys take States."

Bryan looked quickly to Clare, but she was studying John.

"And if they don't?"

"Don't?" John asked. "Don't take States? I don't see that happening considering that we have the new-generation James on the team." He winked at Bryan. Clare saw it and her mouth tightened even more.

"I meant if they don't agree to mediation," she explained.

John put the rule book down on the desk and leaned over a folding chair, gripping the back in both hands. "Allie's membership in the league would be deactivated."

"She'd be kicked out?" She raised her eyebrows. "Just like that?"

John nodded. "We haven't been able to find any wiggle room on that one."

Bryan wanted to say something, but Danny beat him to it.

"I know you have concerns, Clare, but we, well, we've watched Allie grow up here at the rink, and we know she'll be able to work things out with Tim. He'll be as much a part of things as she is before too long."

Clare looked at the wall of photos behind the desk and

then scanned Danny's and John's face. Bryan couldn't tell what she was thinking. It didn't matter, if she'd just say yes. He had issues with the idea of mediation, but he couldn't watch Allie have one more thing taken away. She needed hockey.

Clare picked her bag up without a hint of reconciliation in her posture. If anything, she looked more distant than she had when he walked in. Even when they'd been arguing, at least she'd been engaged.

They were losing her.

"I appreciate that you've explained this all to me, especially the part about States and Allie's eligibility."

John smiled as if they had this in the bag, but he was wrong. They'd made her mad—she wasn't getting ready to say yes, she was ready to walk.

"I have a few questions," she said. "John, you also have a child on Tim's team, is that correct?"

"Jack is the goalie."

"And without Allie the team will have a difficult time making it to the state championship? In fact, they might not make it at all?"

John nodded slowly. Even he was starting to catch on that Clare wasn't falling into line with the plan.

"Thank you for your time," she said. "I'll be in touch."

As she left the room, she brushed close by him. Their arms touched and even though he held himself perfectly still, she flinched away from the contact.

Almost before the door closed behind her, John lifted his hands, confusion written on his soft features. "What just happened?"

"She knows it's a setup," Bryan said. "Why did you bring up States?"

"But—"

Bryan couldn't stay to hear John's next brilliant speech. He closed the door behind him, hoping John and Danny and all their helpful information about the state tournament and how much everyone in the league liked Allie would stay inside. He had to try to salvage this. He was positive if she said no once she wouldn't change her mind. Clare wouldn't flip-flop.

"Clare, wait," he said. "Please." She was closer to the door than to him and he wouldn't have been surprised if she kept right on going, but she stopped. He let his earlier irritation with her and his impatience with the league and the rules go, and he centered on this exact moment.

She stood watching him, one hand clasped around the strap of her backpack, but her eyes were sharp behind her glasses. Sharp, smart and wary.

The door opened behind him and he heard Danny or John, one of them come out into the lobby. He didn't turn, just said, "Can you give us a minute here, guys? Alone?"

The door closed again with a click that echoed in the empty lobby.

Keep track of the facts. One: she stopped. He had a shot. Two: she hadn't called the police last night when she'd had the chance. She must be reluctant to take things that far. Three: even though he'd never had a librarian fantasy before today, he kept wondering what she'd look like if he ever got the opportunity to take off those glasses.

Okay, that last fact was irrelevant, but man, did she push his buttons.

"Thanks for waiting," he said. "I appreciate this."

Sales 101. Give the other person something. Make them think you're the good guy.

Clare didn't acknowledge his thanks. It was as if she hadn't heard him. All right. Get the other person to agree to something. Anything at all. After the first yes, the second would come easier.

"We can both agree that mediation is a good option. It will allow Allie to make amends."

Clare wasn't ready to agree with him yet, not even about that. She came right back at him. "Does she want to make amends?"

"I'm here trying to work that out, aren't I?" *Calm down.* Losing your temper with the other person was a quick way to lose the deal. "Allie will sign on for the mediation," he added. "I'll get her there, but it's no good without Tim."

"Listen, Bryan, that meeting didn't exactly inspire confidence. What it looked like was a bunch of guys who grew up together trying to figure out the best deal for Allie and the team the league president's kid happens to also be on."

He nodded. "I was afraid that was what it looked like."

"What?"

He'd caught her off guard. She probably hadn't expected him to break ranks. He sifted through his options, looking for the sales pitch that was going to work on her.

It was no use. They were talking about kids here, not warm-up jackets. He didn't want to sell her.

He met her eyes and said, "I didn't ask for any of that. It's just, a small town like this, when you grow up together, you stick together, sometimes even if you shouldn't. It's worse with me and hockey because, well, you saw the pictures in there. I made it to a level most guys don't."

"So everyone around here hands you what you want?"

He blew out a breath. "Believe me, if they were giving me what I want, it wouldn't be this." He paced a few steps away but came back. "Allie needs hockey, Clare. I need her to have it. What I told you about her mom, that's only the start of what she's dealing with. Hockey is about the only thing that's working right for her now."

"I'm sorry about that, Bryan. I can see that you're doing what you think is best, but I have to consider Tim. He wants to play hockey for some reason I can't understand. And he says whatever is going on between him and Allie isn't as bad as it looks."

He nodded, encouraging her to keep talking.

"But I'm his mom and I have to remember what really happened." She pointed to the still-broken window of the skate shop across the lobby. The glass was cleaned up, but there was yellow caution tape roping off the window frame. "She beat him up, Bryan. How can I keep exposing him to the same risks?"

She was right, he realized, chilled by the thought. They were beyond John hoping his kid could play on a state-championship team.

"You guessed they cooked up this mediation plan just to keep Allie on the team," he said. "And you're probably right, in John's case." He hesitated but then decided she ought to know everything. If he wanted her to trust him, he had to trust her. "The truth is, Allie shouldn't be playing for Twin Falls. I'm not bragging, I'm telling you the deal. She's been playing on a select travel team the last couple years, but with her mom gone and my work schedule, I couldn't work out the logistics to get her to the practices and games this season. This is probably the only time she'll be playing with these kids again and John wants that state trophy from her."

He rubbed his forehead. This wasn't the kind of thing parents normally said out loud even if they all knew it was true. He searched her eyes, hoping he'd see some hint there that she understood.

"I'm asking you to forget about John and States and that this solution probably wouldn't be on the table if he didn't want Allie on the team. I'm asking you to give mediation a chance anyway. Danny says the lady is good and—" He hesitated. "Allie needs help. With the team on the line as a condition, I can make her go talk to this mediator."

It was one of the hardest things he'd ever said, but with the caution tape in the empty window of the skate shop staring him in the face, he was out of options.

She cleared her throat. She hated that he'd stopped trying to sell her. This was exactly why she didn't want anything to do with mediation. As Lila had explained it this morning, the point of mediation was getting to know people and starting to care about their problems. She didn't want to hear the pain in his voice or see the panic in his eyes every time he caught a glimpse of the broken window.

"I appreciate you being so honest, Bryan," she said. "But I'm afraid the answer is still no."

His mouth twisted and he glanced over his shoulder toward the office. "I hope to hell John can't hear us," he muttered. He started to reach for her and then pulled back. "Sorry. But can we move?" he asked. "I wouldn't put it past him to be listening at the door."

"Bryan, I have a full day scheduled. I'm going to go."

"I swear you're going to want to hear this," he said.

She took a deep breath and then followed him as he walked toward the far corner of the lobby.

"You're missing the big picture," he said. "If Allie doesn't go through the mediation, she's off the team, right?"

She nodded.

"John's kid doesn't get to States then, right?"

She nodded again.

"John's not the only one counting on Allie to bring this home. There are a whole bunch of other seventh graders on that team and all of their parents in the bleachers. This is a hockey town."

"Tim told me. It's why he wants to play."

"So when Allie gets kicked off the team for fighting, what do you imagine happens to Tim?"

Wow.

For a person who got paid to connect the dots in logic situations, she'd certainly missed the boat on this one.

"He'll be crucified," she said quietly.

Bryan closed his eyes and let out his breath. "It sucks, Clare, but yeah."

She pulled the strap of her bag tighter across her chest. She wished like hell she'd never heard of Twin Falls or that the savings bank hadn't experienced a security breach. She wished she could blame Bryan, but he hadn't wanted to have to spell this out. He wasn't holding it over her head in a power play, he was telling her what he knew about this team and his town. About these people who were going to back Allie without question because she was a James and she'd grown up here and they all wanted to win this tournament. If he was right, and she had no doubt he was, he'd just saved Tim a world of problems.

When Tim asked to stop moving around, was he hoping for what Bryan and Allie had? To be an inextricable part of someone's life? To not have to earn his way in again because he was already there?

"What a disaster," she said. "I don't even care about hockey. I just want Tim to be happy."

"That's a big goal," he said.

"What is?"

"Being happy."

Having seen the difference between young Bryan and the guy standing in front of her, she wondered when someone had last made it their goal to make him happy.

"I appreciate the time you took to explain things to me. I'm going to consider everything you said."

He surprised her by smiling. "I guess if you did decide to go with mediation we might not be so bad at it, huh?"

"Maybe not," she agreed. His smiled deepened.

She walked away quickly, not wanting to be drawn any further into his plans. It was bad enough that she didn't really have any options left. She didn't want to complicate things even more by falling for his smile.

HE WAS IN HIS BEDROOM that night, folding a load of laundry. He'd left it in the dryer for most of the week and everything was hopelessly wrinkled.

When the phone rang, he dropped the T-shirt he'd

been trying to smooth and dived for the receiver—he'd talk to a telemarketer if it meant he didn't have to deal with another wrinkled shirt.

"Hello?"

"We'll do it." He recognized Clare's voice. "I'm not sure it's a good idea, but we'll do it."

"Thank you," he said.

"I…uh…I know you didn't have to tell me what would happen to Tim if I didn't let him go to mediation. After the things I said about Allie…I want to thank you."

"I wasn't being unselfish, you know."

"I've been thinking about when you said wanting someone to be happy is a big goal," she continued quietly. "It is. But I still want it."

When he said that, he'd been talking about Erin. He'd tried to give her what she wanted—a home, some cash in the bank account, a kid—and she'd told him if she didn't get out of their marriage she was going to go crazy. Being married to him had been the thing that made her life suck. So yeah. It was all well and good to say you wanted someone to be happy, but to actually make it your goal to make them get happy and stay that way? *Good freaking luck.*

Which didn't change the fact that he was trying like hell to make Allie happy.

He sat down on the bed and the stack of folded shirts tipped over behind him, falling onto the floor. "Me, too."

"So that makes two out of the four of us with the same agenda. Maybe this will work."

"Maybe," he answered. After she hung up, he scooped the laundry back onto the bed and picked up the first shirt to refold. "Maybe."

CHAPTER FIVE

CLARE PUSHED THE DOOR to the family room open with her hip while she wrapped a scarf around her neck. The last time she complained about the weather, Lindsey sent her the scarf, along with an enormous Russian-style fur hat, which Tim had appropriated for a snowman. The luscious turquoise and rich brown combination of yarn reminded her of her friend every time she wore it.

Tim was sprawled in a red corduroy beanbag chair, headphones on, hands furiously working the controller for his Xbox.

"Can you pause the game?" Clare asked. For a second she wondered if he'd heard her, but then he tossed the controller on the floor next to his chair.

"You're really going?" he asked.

"Really going," she said. "Why?"

He stood and stretched, his fingertips inches away from the low ceiling in the family room. His eye was still bruised and slightly swollen, but other than that, the effects of the fight had faded. "I don't know. We've been here for three months and this is the first time you're going out. Usually by now you'd be in a book club, signed up for classes in random hobby number forty-seven and working on your second date with some poor guy. I thought you were on strike."

"On strike from what?"

"Meeting people."

"Why would you say that?"

"Because I want to stay and you want to prove to me that it sucks here."

"You don't really mean that, do you?"

"Well, why aren't you joining stuff?"

He was too sharp for his own good sometimes. Or was it for her good? She didn't know why she had been dragging her feet, but he was right. She wasn't getting the charge out of Twin Falls that she normally got when they landed somewhere new.

Partly it was not wanting to leave him alone at night. Her job was more stressful than normal because the bank manager wasn't used to dealing with technology and he kept second-guessing her recommendations. They needed to move ahead faster because her contract had a hard deadline when the board of directors met again in May. But the truth was, she hadn't felt the energy she usually did in a new place. Was she finally burned out on new beginnings? She honestly didn't know.

"Three months hardly makes me a hermit," she said sharply. He looked surprised and she regretted her tone. It wasn't Tim's fault she was out of step. "I've just been waiting for the perfect invite."

"And a kickboxing class full of mothers you've never met on a snowy night is the perfect invite?" He shook his head. "Thought you only liked to work out alone. Like a ninja." He threw a couple karate chops at the air.

"I'm changing my habits. Becoming more of a marine."

"Right."

He waited.

"Fine. The truth is, I'm going tonight because I

couldn't come up with an excuse fast enough when Mrs. Crandall asked." Clare shrugged. "She doesn't seem like a person who's used to taking no for an answer."

He flopped back into the beanbag and picked up his controller. "Neither is her daughter."

"What does that mean?"

"Nothing."

"Nothing?"

"Bye, Mom." His attention was already back on the screen. She wasn't going to get any more information out of him at this point. She'd have to remember to see what she could find out from Mary Crandall about this "daughter" situation.

"I'll be home by nine at the latest. Lock the door after I leave, okay? Call my cell if you're looking for me."

His fingers flew on the controller. "Got it. Try not to kick anybody where the sun doesn't shine."

She leaned down and kissed the top of his head. "I'll attempt to control myself."

SHE PULLED HER PRIUS into a spot outside the low, forest-green shingled building with the sign outside that identified it as the City Fitness Center. Clare stared through the window at the snow blowing across the lot. There were exactly two other cars there.

City. Hah.

She'd never lived this far north and, in her opinion, the weather was overdone. A touch less snow and a tad more sun wouldn't degrade the winter experience. It would still be freezing, snowy and inhospitable, but a small reduction from arctic to plain-old-cold would go a long way toward making her want to get out of her car so she could go inside and exercise.

She wished she could muster interest in meeting these new women, but Tim had been right. No matter how often she told herself she should start making an effort, a part of her fought back. If they were only here through the end of May, what was the point?

It unsettled her that she felt so little interest, but it didn't change her feeling that if she'd been able to get out of Mary's invitation tonight, she would be home doing her workout in the privacy of her own bedroom. She was going to have to force herself through the hour somehow.

Luckily the City Club only allowed two visits on a guest pass before you had to join so she could plead poverty at that point if she hated the class or the people. She glanced out the window again. Still snowing.

In the end, she only left the car because she was there early enough to get in a weight routine before the class. With only two guest visits, she didn't want to waste one.

She put a fresh coat of lip gloss on as protection against the wind before grabbing her bag and opening the car door to a blast of frigid air.

Ugh. How did people who grew up here not move to Arizona as soon as they graduated high school?

The parking lot was slippery in the bare spots and calf deep where snow had drifted with the wind, and she was glad she'd worn her good boots as she turned her face into the collar of her coat and hurried toward the door.

THE CHANGE ROOM was deserted. There was an open gym bag in front of one locker, but that was the only sign anyone was in the building. Clare wondered if the kickboxing class had been canceled because of the snow. After she changed into her yoga pants and T-shirt, she stopped at the information desk. The kid behind the counter was wearing headphones, but he pulled them off and reassured her that the class was still on. He was probably lonely.

"We don't shut down unless the state police close the roads for a snow emergency," he told her. "Doesn't happen more than once or twice a winter, usually."

Perfect. Only two snow emergencies a year. She shivered as she thanked him and put her own earbuds in.

There were three people in the weight room when she pushed the door open. Two women were chatting as they used a leg machine. Clare steered away from them toward a treadmill where she could start with a quick warm-up. She glanced at the guy on the first treadmill, intending to make friendly, but not too friendly, eye contact.

The guy on the treadmill was Bryan James.

Bryan James had a fantastic body.

He didn't see her and she didn't know if she was disappointed about that as she stepped onto a treadmill down the line from his.

The mirrors stretching across the front of the room presented her with a dilemma. If she looked in the mirrors she was in danger of him noticing her and then having to talk to him. On the other hand, if she kept her head down, she would miss her chance for another look at his body.

She'd broken up with her last boyfriend, Vince, a few weeks before she moved. That meant it had been more than four months since she'd last had a good look at a guy. Vince had been handsome enough, but he'd have faded into the wallpaper next to Bryan.

Tim had been right earlier when he said she liked to have a guy around to date. She made sure they knew she wasn't interested in long-term and most of the time, the men she dated were fine with that. If they weren't, she politely bowed out and found another guy who was. Since she'd been in Twin Falls, most of the guys she'd met were married. None of the others had whet her interest. Except one.

She watched the display on her treadmill, holding out for a count of fifty-seven seconds before she snuck a peek. She was so weak. Not even a minute. But, oh, was her weakness well rewarded!

Red shorts and a navy T-shirt. Nothing mesh or spandex. Firm in all the right places. The exact broad-shoulder-to-slim-waist proportion she liked the best. Very nice. Eyes back on her display, she managed to wait another minute before she looked again. This time she lingered.

He was reading a magazine as he ran and while his attention was on turning the page, she noted that he'd worked up enough of a sweat that his shirt was clinging to his back and his abs. Was that what hockey players looked like under their pads? If so, why did they bother with the pads?

She studied her display to try to figure out how to change the incline. Ten seconds was all it took to create a slight increase in height of the treadmill slope. The new angle meant that she could get a better view of his legs if she leaned forward like...

"Oh," she gasped as she saw the mess of scar tissue

covering his knee. She instinctively looked back to his face, hoping he hadn't heard her.

No such luck, she thought as she raised a hand in a pathetic attempt at a nonchalant wave. He'd heard. He looked at her, no hint of recognition, no nothing. For one agonizing second, while she held her hand up, he stared and then he looked away.

She remembered what it had been like to go out with Gretchen in her wheelchair. Everyone stared and then turned away fast, but not fast enough. They were constantly confronted with the uncomfortable knowledge that absolutely every person they met wanted to know what was wrong with her sister when all her sister wanted was to be ordinary.

She was ashamed enough over being caught staring that she was able to keep her eyes on her machine as she finished her warm-up. It didn't matter how cute he was, he was Allie's dad. If she could have kept that in her mind, she could have avoided this embarrassment.

He was still running when she turned off her treadmill and crossed to the bench behind her to start her first set of lifts.

She adjusted the weight and then settled into place. She put a hand on her thigh and felt the muscle contract under her fingers as she worked. What could have happened to Bryan's knee to cause the damage she'd seen? It looked as if the injury started on his thigh and the scarring trailed down his knee onto his shin. It could have been a burn. Whatever caused it, she understood why he walked with a hint of a limp. She was surprised it wasn't a lot worse.

She closed her eyes and pushed herself more than usual, wishing she could lose herself in the rhythm of her breathing, in the clank of the weights, in anything except fantasies about Bryan James.

When her first set was over, she opened her eyes and sat up. He was standing close to the edge of the bench.

"Small world," he said.

The dark color of his shirt brought out the blue in his eyes and the exercise had put just enough red in his cheeks to draw her attention. Johnny Depp circa *21 Jump Street* had given her a lifelong love affair with excellent cheekbones. Bryan was the first guy she'd met who could give Johnny a run for his money.

"Yes, it is," she answered. He'd pulled a pair of track pants on over his shorts. She was determined to make up for her bad manners and to prove to herself that she was capable of ignoring her body's base instincts.

She forced herself to relax, leaning back on the bench, pretending they often met to chat about exercise. "Is it always so quiet in here?"

"There's a kickboxing class in about half an hour that pulls a good crowd. This is more quiet than usual. It's cold tonight."

She smiled. "I'm so glad you said that. I was beginning to feel like a wimp."

"You're not used to snow?"

She swung her legs around and faced him. "I've lived in eleven cities in eight states, but I've never been this far north before. I have to say, not impressed."

"It's just snow. Nothing personal."

"When I got out of my car and the wind came up inside my coat, it felt personal."

He laughed.

He had a really nice laugh. It changed his face completely. Wiped away the worry and stress.

He had crinkles at the corners of his eyes that made her think he'd done quite a bit of laughing. And the way his eyes sparkled, she couldn't help smiling. She wished she could tell another joke and make him laugh again.

He was giving her a sideways glance as he fiddled with the half zipper on his pullover jacket. The stripes on the sleeves made his shoulders look even more impossibly broad. Then he tilted his head and she could suddenly see that wicked promise she'd first noticed in his college photo. She wasn't thinking about making him laugh anymore.

She swallowed.

She crossed her legs.

The kickboxers better get here quick before she did something embarrassing like pushing those other women out the door, locking it behind them, and having her way with a hockey stud right here in this room with all the mirrors.

CLARE HAD A SENSE of humor. He hadn't expected that. He'd seen her staring at his knee and he'd come over to say something, something to let her know he'd seen her.

His knee was a mess. He could have had plastic surgery, gotten the scarring cleaned up some, but he'd wanted it to stay ugly so he wouldn't forget. He never wanted to forget how stupid he'd been, how arrogant, and how his own bad choices had screwed up his knee, his career and ultimately his family. There'd been a time when he bought into the idea that he was one of the charmed ones and he'd lost sight of the reality that he was exactly like everyone else. No more or less entitled to luck.

He knew what his knee was—he lived with it. He didn't need Clare looking at it and pitying him. He didn't want her pity. Didn't want her to know him. The less she learned about him or Allie, the better.

He'd meant to tell her something like that but she'd surprised him by being so...human.

The last thing he needed was to find out that he liked Clare. Their situation was complicated enough.

She coughed and lifted her water bottle to drink. She had a good profile and with her chin up and the long muscles of her throat exposed, he wondered if she'd ever been a dancer. She took a long swallow from the bottle and he licked his lips. How could a woman's neck have him this turned on?

They were in a weight room, for Pete's sake.

But she was wearing a tight top and he could see the sweet curve of her breasts and he was having trouble remembering why he'd been mad at her in the first place.

Lord help him.

She lowered the water bottle when the door from the hall opened and a knot of women came in. His sister, Mary, crossed the room with a big smile on her face while the other women moved toward the dance studio where the kickboxing class was held.

"Clare, you came!" Mary was wearing black pants and a lime-green tank with a black stripe. She patted Clare's arm and then slipped her own arm around Bryan. "I see you met my brother."

"Bryan? He's your brother?"

"Sure is." Mary squeezed his waist and then pulled away. "Yuck. You're sweaty."

"I'm at the gym. I'm supposed to be sweaty," he said. How did Mary know Clare?

"It's still gross."

"I wonder what I did to deserve such a kind and loving big sister?"

Mary swatted him, smirking at Clare. "He loves to remind me that I'm over forty."

"Hey, I said 'big,' not 'old.'"

Mary rolled her eyes. "You better watch yourself, Bryan. I kickbox." She faced Clare. "So, before class starts and I'm too out of breath to talk, I'm under strict orders from my daughter to find out your son's birthday."

"His birthday?"

"Apparently your son is the cutest boy in seventh grade. Lisa is having a few girls over on Friday night and in order for them to properly forecast which of them will wind up marrying him...Tim, right?"

Bryan hoped Mary couldn't tell that he was pissed. Allie used to be invited to Lisa's sleepovers. He wondered who the other girls were and why Allie was left out.

"That's right," Mary said. "They want Tim's birth date for some vital astrology work."

Clare burst out laughing. "On Tim? Tim is the cutest boy in seventh grade?"

Mary nodded. "Lisa wrote a poem about his hair. Is it possible his hair could be described as a 'fringe of shimmering gold'?"

"If that means it's dirty blond and hangs in his eyes, then yes."

Mary smiled. "I've got the right boy, then. Bryan, has Allie met this most perfect seventh grader?"

He couldn't laugh with them. Whatever was going on with Allie meant she wasn't part of this joke. "They met."

"So is Allie writing poems, too?" —

Bryan twisted the towel he was holding in an effort to keep his voice calm. He did not want Clare to know how upset he was. He owed it to Allie to make it seem as if he was fine with everything.

"Tim is the kid Allie fought with. We're doing community mediation instead of poetry readings."

Mary's face was red. "I'm so sorry. I had no idea Tim was...that Allie had...that you—"

Clare cut her off before she could stammer herself in a circle. "It's okay, Mary. We're working it out."

When she met his eye, he thought he saw pity again. He did not want her pity, not for him and certainly not for Allie.

"I have to get home. Enjoy your class."

It was abrupt, but it was the best he could manage. He could call Mary later and apologize. Or not. Maybe he'd call her and ask her exactly when Lisa stopped inviting Allie to sleepovers.

He didn't shower, just threw his clothes into his bag and headed out into the cold. When the wind hit his face, he remembered Clare's joke about the snow and his immediate jump to what it would feel like to get his hands up under her coat.

Stupid.

The only thing he needed from Clare was a certificate of completion when the mediation was over.

Once they got through this, Allie could go back to

her hockey team. Tim and the rest of the seventh grade could get on with their poetry and their sleepovers. And he could get on with his life. Whatever that was going to be.

CLARE BRUSHED HER HAND across the surface of the bench after Bryan walked away. Mary looked so embarrassed that she felt sorry for the woman.

"You didn't know," Clare said.

"I didn't mean to upset him. He's been having such a hard time," Mary said. She sounded as if she might go on, but Clare jumped in.

"You don't have to explain. It's fine."

"I shouldn't have mentioned the sleepover. Allie and Lisa used to be close, but this year has been difficult. She's not invited. I was so excited about Tim, but I shouldn't have said anything in front of my brother."

Clare stood up. "I'm sure it's okay."

Mary obviously meant well, but she didn't want to talk about Bryan with his sister. She didn't want him to hear that she was prying into his business behind his back. It felt important to her that they'd managed to make a small bridge between them.

"We should head into class," she said.

They walked to the studio together, both quiet. When they reached the door, she remembered what Mary had said about Tim. She couldn't help feeling a little thrill for him. "January twenty-fourth," she said. "Tim's an Aquarius."

"The girls will be delighted."

Tim was a heartthrob now? When had that happened?

CHAPTER SIX

ALLIE WAS FURIOUS WITH HIM. John was so far past furious with him it would be funny if it weren't so depressing. He'd gotten dirty looks from almost every parent on the team. Bryan felt like crap, but he was damn sure he'd done the right thing.

He glanced at the box again. Allie, in her jersey, but no pads, no skates, no helmet, had her arms crossed, a scowl on her face. There was an empty space between her and the next kid on the bench.

A defenseman from the visiting team took the puck on a breakaway and shot. The horn blew, announcing another goal. The Cowboys were losing four-zip in the first period while their best player rode the bench.

He leaned against the glass, wishing the clock would move faster so they could end the torture for everyone. Warm air hit the back of his neck when the lobby door opened and he turned to see Clare coming in. Hesitantly she walked toward him. She wore the collar turned up on her coat and with the dark fabric framing her face her eyes shone an even richer dark brown.

"I was in the car. I got hung up with a call from work," she said. "I guess I missed some of the game." She checked the scoreboard. "Oops. That's not good."

"It's one game in a long season." He'd already heard

similar comments from everyone connected with the team and he was out of patience.

"Sorry," she said.

The action moved away from them down the ice and Clare started to edge away toward the bleachers where the other parents were sitting. She stopped after a few steps, her attention on the players' box.

"Is Allie hurt?" she asked.

"Benched."

A pink blush rose up from her neck to her cheeks. "Because of the fight? I didn't know the league was going to—"

"They didn't. I told John to sit her out."

Clare looked confused. "You did?"

"She beat up a teammate," he said. "She has to learn she can't get away with things like that."

Two Cowboys slammed one of the wings from the other team into the boards right in front of Clare and she jumped. A stick clattered against the glass and then the play moved around behind the goal.

"I'm never going to get used to that," she said.

"It's more fun than it looks."

"I imagine professional bullfighters would say the same thing, but I'm not inclined to believe them, either."

There it was again. On the surface prissy, but underneath that quirky humor.

"I imagine," he agreed.

The horn went off for another goal at almost the same time as the whistle blew to end the period.

"Want to sit down?" she asked, gesturing with her elbow toward the other parents.

"I better not antagonize them with my presence."

Her phone rang and she pulled it out and then opened it. "Did you get the test files loaded?" she asked. She paused and then said, "Give me a minute and I'll call you back."

She closed the phone and put it back in her pocket. "I guess I'm headed back out to the car." She looked over at the bench. "She's out for the whole game?"

He nodded. He waited for her to pipe up with a comment like every other parent he'd talked to this morning. She didn't. Maybe that was why he offered her an explanation.

"If you get away with everything, you stop worrying about consequences," he said. "I don't want her getting hurt later because no one drew a line now."

She touched his arm lightly. "She'll be fine." Then she nudged him. "Even John will forgive you," she said. "Eventually."

He stood there by the glass for the rest of the game. He could have sat with the other parents. Clare was right; they'd forgive him. But instead he waited by himself, watching Allie, not really paying attention to the game, and thinking about Clare. Of all the parents on the team, she was the only one with a justifiable reason to be involved in Allie's discipline, but she was the only one who hadn't jumped in with her two cents. Every time he thought he knew what to expect from her, she surprised him.

"LINDSEY, PAY ATTENTION," Clare said. It was early Monday morning and they were on a video call consulting on her outfit for the meeting with the mediator. "I have to look right today."

On her computer screen, Clare could see that Lindsey

was reclined all the way back in her black leather office chair, her feet crossed at the ankle on the corner of her mahogany desk. The red-and-black color scheme, brass accents and substantial furniture she'd chosen made Clare picture Michael Douglas in *Wall Street*. Lindsey loved that her desk was bigger than her lawyer father's. She said she hadn't actually measured, but Clare wasn't sure she believed her. Her friend might be overinvested in image, but that only increased her value as a fashion consultant.

"I don't get why you're trying so hard," Lindsey said. "That little creep beat Tim up. She's wrong, he's right. You could show up in a mu-mu and you'd still have the high ground."

Clare did a slow turn in front of her computer camera. She smoothed her hands down the gray cardigan and black pleated skirt. "How's this?"

Lindsey tapped a finger on her chin. "Are you going for seventy-year-old sexually frustrated middle school principal?"

"Lindsey!"

"What? I'm trying to get the intended outcomes down."

"You're supposed to be helping me."

"You want my help? Don't wear that outfit. Ever."

Clare threw herself onto her bed. "I hate that we're doing this."

"Doing what? Helping that girl keep her spot on the hockey team?" Lindsey threw a foam basketball at the screen of her computer. "You should have said no."

"I told you, that would have ruined things for Tim with the team."

"What's his sudden interest in hockey about, anyway?"

"What basketball was to our school, hockey is here," Clare said. "Plus, it's a very dramatic sport. Lots of banging and speed."

"I can see Tim loving that. He's never been the shy type."

"I don't know how I ended up with this kid who loves chaos. I'm in computer security, Matteo is a business analyst. By all rights, Tim should be playing chess."

"Don't make it sound like Matteo's genes ever stood a chance. That kid is all yours."

Clare pretended she couldn't hear. If her computer had been on a Clapper, she'd have clapped it off.

"You're lying anyway," Lindsey said. "You like his chaos even if you're too mature to make waves yourself. Something else is bugging you. Look at me."

Clare pulled a pillow over her face. Lindsey knew her inside and out, which was a comfort except when it was an inconvenience.

She heard a loud tapping and lifted the edge of the pillow to see Lindsey knocking on her camera lens. "*Wait.* Is the hockey dad cute?"

Clare pulled the pillow back down. She held it tightly clamped to her face while she shook her head and tried not to think about how good he'd looked stripped down to a single layer of T-shirt and shorts in the gym the other night. She muttered, "Hideous."

"You're lying again. Even through a computer monitor, I can *smell* you lying."

"Why would I lie?"

"When," Lindsey asked, "did you first realize you wanted to hook up with a hockey dad?"

She was suffocating. She dropped the pillow and stood up so she could change while they talked.

"I don't want to hook up with him," Clare said. "The problem is that I haven't had sex since I broke up with Vince so my judgment is clouded by hormones. This hiatus from sex has triggered one of those survival-of-the-species instincts from back before humans had fire."

"You're having cavewoman feelings?" Lindsey uncrossed her legs and sat forward. "A mating instinct? For a hockey guy? Please tell me he has all his teeth?"

Clare shoved the black skirt off and pulled on a pair of dark blue jeans. "He has all his teeth." *And a very nice smile.*

"Those jeans are perfect."

"I'll wear my boots. Then if Bryan tries to intimidate me with that big-jock thing he does where he takes up all the space, I'll be tall, too."

"That's good," Lindsey agreed. "Tall and in charge on bottom. What about on top? Same thing or are we sending a more complex and layered message?"

"I want to seem approachable."

"Approachable or doable?"

"*Approachable.* For the mediator, Lindsey. I want her to look at me and know I'm a good mom."

"Wear that sweater I got you for Christmas last year. Nothing gives you mommy cred like lilac cashmere. And that particular lilac cashmere also gives you the boobs of a woman raking in the tips at Hooters. Which should make me jealous, but I'm generous enough to be happy for you that your boobs can still pass for twenty-five."

She put the sweater on, smoothed her hair and turned in front of the camera again.

"Sooo much better than the principal outfit. Good mommy with great boobs on top, intimidating tall lady on bottom. That outfit is the perfect combination of nice and don't screw with me." Lindsey clapped. "Now tell me more about this guy you're having the cavewoman-attraction thing with."

"I'm not attracted. Or at least, 'cavewoman' is a little strong. I happened to notice that he's handsome." She sat on the edge of the bed and pulled her laptop closer so she could focus on her friend. "Nothing can happen anyway, so I should let it go."

"Why let it go? Why not have some dates?" Lindsey whined. "I haven't dated a jock since college, but as far as I remember, they're a lot of fun."

Clare shrugged. "His kid is the one that beat Tim up. How can I date him if I don't like his child?"

"That's a problem. When I dated jocks, they weren't dads." Lindsey folded her arms on her desk and stared seriously into the screen. "I don't like his kid, either. But he's cute?"

"Too cute for his own good, screwed up emotionally and he has a problem child. He's like a man-to-avoid trifecta." She got up to dig out a pair of earrings from the basket on her dresser. She had opal studs that would look good with the sweater. She remembered his knee. "Plus, he has a tragic past. Definitely not boyfriend material."

And he was the hometown hockey hero—the very definition of Twin Falls native. Dating him would mean she would be automatically integrated into the fabric of the town. If Tim thought there was a chance she was interested in Bryan, he'd launch a full-court press, or whatever they called the equivalent move in hockey, to make sure they got together. He'd see it as a chance to persuade her to stay.

"I have to see this for myself. Full name? First and last?" Lindsey asked.

"Bryan James."

She heard Lindsey tapping her keyboard and spun around. "You are not looking him up on the Internet."

"Oh, yes, I am. Huh, he's Bryan with a *y?* That's sweet. Let's just enlarge this." Lindsey tapped her keyboard. "Holy Hot Hockey Players. My God. Wow."

Clare edged closer to her laptop. "I'm guessing you found a picture?"

Her instant-message box pinged. Lindsey had sent her a link. When the page opened, there was Bryan. *Holy Hot Hockey Players, indeed.*

It was a picture from his college days and his shoulders looked impossibly broad in the shoulder pads and uniform jersey. His face had fewer lines and his hair was longer. The thing that caught her attention, though, was his smile and his eyes. He was turned half to the side, laughing over his shoulder at the photographer. It was the same smile from the little-kid-hockey picture she'd seen on Danny's wall. The smile she'd seen so briefly when they'd been together in the gym that night before Mary came.

She wanted to see if she could make him smile again. She wished she didn't want that, but she did. To see the worry lift, to know she'd done that for him, well, she wanted it again.

She was gradually, begrudgingly, being convinced that he was a good guy. Benching Allie when even her coaches wanted her to play had taken a special kind of guts. When you loved your kid enough that you'd rather see them sad than let them keep on doing something that was hurting them, she knew how hard that was. When she first met Allie and Bryan, she'd never have guessed he was that type of dad.

"I can see how your inner cavewoman would choose to be involved with him," Lindsey said as she kept clicking. "Jocks, man. When they're handsome and talented, that's proof that the world isn't fair."

"He looks different now."

"Man boobs? Nose ring? Shaved his eyebrows?"

"Tired," she blurted. She glanced at Lindsey and then quickly shut the Web site with Bryan's picture. "I mean, he'd been traveling the first night I met him, and the situation was upsetting. Anyone would have looked tired."

She didn't tell Lindsey about the gym. She felt the same desire to keep it private that she'd had with Mary.

"But you noticed. It stuck with you," Lindsey said.

Clare shrugged.

Lindsey picked up a pencil and started tapping on her desk blotter. "You know, Clare, I can't remember the last time I heard you say something like that about a guy."

"What do you mean?"

"When you met Vince you told me all about his hair and how great he looked in his soccer shorts. Before him, there was Tom and you wouldn't shut up about his perfect back. And who was the one who had the cowboy boots? The one when you always showed up early for dates so you could watch him walk in?"

"Denny."

"Denny with the sexy swagger. That's right." Lindsey

put the pencil down. "Screw it, we've been friends long enough that I can say what I think, right?"

Clare had never wished harder for a quick power outage to shut down the Internet. She nodded.

"Okay. Here it is. You never tell me how you feel about them. Or why you like them outside of bed. And jokes about his bully child aside, you never go for guys with kids of their own. You have this perfect setup where you move every year or so, find a new guy, have some good sex and then leave the guy behind when it's time to go. You and the guy both know going in that it won't last, so it's easy to stay superficial. You set this up as securely as the networks you make for your clients." Lindsey's voice softened and Clare heard the hesitation in it, a foreign sound from her decisive friend. "But this guy, you already seem to care about him."

"I only said he looked tired."

"I know. And I know you can't date him because his daughter is headed for juvie. But don't you ever wonder if you're going to meet a guy who'd tempt you to stay in one place?"

"Did Tim bribe you to talk up his agenda?" Clare snapped a bracelet on her wrist, her voice brisk when she added, "I have a meeting to attend, so I have to go."

"You'll be great, Clare. One of your very best skills is being a mom. You'll know how to handle this because you're doing it for Tim."

"Right," Clare said. "Okay."

"Trust the sweater. Your boobs look perfect."

"I'm counting on the boots. Bryan with a *y* is not a small man."

"Enough," Lindsey said. "One more word about the sexy hockey dad and I'm going to wind up cruising sports bars this weekend when I promised myself I'd clean the bathroom."

After she closed the connection, Clare leaned on her desk for a moment in her bedroom and wondered what it would feel like to settle somewhere, maybe back in Seattle near Lindsey, or even here in Twin Falls where the winter sucked but the men, or at least one man, did not.

She considered how hard she had to work to raise Tim, to keep him happy and safe. What if she were responsible for someone else, too? What if the circle of people she cared about expanded. What if it wasn't just Tim, but Bryan and Allie that she had to worry over.

She shivered. *Scary.* That's how it would feel. Bone-deep scary.

SHE WAS LATER THAN she'd hoped to pick Tim up at school so she got stuck in the congestion of buses and minivans tangling with the kids who walked home from school and who, apparently, were unable to look one way, let alone two ways before crossing the street. Between the snow piled up everywhere, the glare from the unexpectedly bright sun and the kids who seemed determined to throw themselves under her car, she'd had to pay such close attention to not accidentally killing anyone that they were only a few blocks away from the mediator's office when she realized that the peculiar odor she'd noticed in the car was coming from Tim. Was he wearing cologne?

Did Tim *own cologne?*

She sniffed again. Actually, she wasn't even sure the scent was cologne. It was more medicinal than pleasant.

"Did you spill something on yourself?"

"No."

"Well, what's that smell then?"

"I don't smell anything," he muttered. The redness creeping up his neck as he surreptitiously held the collar of his sweatshirt up to his nose and sniffed, told her she'd guessed correctly.

He *was* wearing cologne or maybe that horrible body spray he'd gotten a sample of in his "puberty tool kit" in health class last year. She snuck a closer look at him and realized he'd combed his hair recently, the wet lines showing where he'd taken the time to part it. He'd started wearing it longer that summer and the thick bangs he brushed across his forehead made his eyes look even bigger than normal.

Golden fringe, indeed.

She shifted her hands on the steering wheel, checked the road and then stole another peek at him. He was staring out his window and was quiet, much too quiet for Tim. Normally by the time he got out of school, he was so wound up he could talk her ear off quoting conversations from the lunch room verbatim just to let out the energy he had to work so hard to control in class.

"Anything you want to talk about?"

"No." He pushed the button to recline his seat, crossed his skinny arms on his jacket and closed his eyes. "I'm taking a nap."

Less than half a minute later, she pulled into a parking space and turned the car off.

"Sorry to disturb your sleep, but we're here."

"Great." He had the door open and one foot on the ground practically before the engine was off. "I wasn't tired anyway."

He walked ahead of her toward the building and she studied him from behind. The sun was out and she was in no hurry to get inside the center. He was still an inch shorter than her, but to her mother's eye he seemed impossibly tall. He had a slender frame with long legs that gave him a gangly grace. From her perspective, he'd always been adorable. Did this sudden flurry of personal grooming mean he was hoping to find out if girls his own age also found him adorable?

Bryan and Allie had gotten there first and were sitting on opposite sides of the small, musty-smelling waiting room. Tim hesitated in the doorway and then took the seat next to Allie who shifted so she was pressed against the arm of her chair, as far away from him as she could get.

It looked as if at least one seventh-grade girl was not a fan of Tim and his special cologne.

Clare sat next to Bryan. "The traffic at school was crazy," she said. "I'm amazed I didn't run anyone over."

"It's the sun," he said. "You get a nice day like this in November and it makes everyone a little nuts."

She noticed that he'd leaned toward her and taken a subtle sniff. "Yes, there is a weird smell in the room," she muttered. "But it's not me. I swear."

"It's Tim," Allie said. "He's wearing perfume."

Clare's eyes shot to her son. Instead of being embarrassed, he flexed his shoulders and said, "It's not perfume. It's Axe. And it's beast."

Allie rolled her eyes but Clare was surprised that for a second there she actually looked less tense. Her perfectly ordinary disgust with everyone in her vicinity was reassuringly normal. For the first time she thought this might work.

Bryan mouthed the word *beast* at her and raised his eyebrows.

"*Beast* is this generation's *rad*."

"Groovy," he said.

Lila came out of her office through a door near Allie's chair. "The kids and I have a few things to sort out before we're ready for you. Will you wait here? We shouldn't take more than fifteen minutes."

Tim stood quickly, following Lila down the hall toward a conference room. Allie was holding the end of her braid in one hand, nervously flicking it back and forth between her fingers. "You coming, Allie?" Tim called.

Allie blushed, her eyes flicking to Clare and then to the corridor where Tim was holding a door open for her. "Dad, I really don't want to."

Bryan said, "It might not be so bad."

"But—"

He crossed the room and crouched in front of his daughter. If Clare could have figured out how to leave the room without making the situation more awkward, she would have. Bryan put his hands over Allie's and gently tugged the braid out of her fingers. He leaned in and whispered.

"It's going to be all right, kiddo."

"Why can't I just apologize?"

Bryan shifted his shoulders. He was trying to give Allie some privacy.

"This is what everyone decided was best." He lifted their linked hands, encouraging her. "You want me to walk down there with you?"

Allie shook her head. She pulled her hands out of his grasp, laying them flat on her knees before standing up and walking down the short hall.

Clare didn't know what to say. If she hadn't been there the night Allie fought with Tim, she would never have believed the girl who'd been sitting across from her was capable of any kind of violence. Allie looked sad, not dangerous.

He slapped his hands on the arm of the chair in front of him and pushed himself up.

"I was in the car the whole day. I can't believe I'm stuck here while the sun is shining outside." He seemed to be trying to pretend the past few minutes had never happened. Clare was more than happy to accommodate him.

"I can't even imagine Twin Falls in the summer—I feel as if it's been covered in snow since we moved here."

"Just wait," Bryan said. He was facing the door to the parking lot, his head tilted back, basking in the weak rays shining through the blinds. "Summer is gorgeous."

"Too bad we won't be here," she said.

He half turned. "You what?"

"I'm a freelancer. My contract at the bank is up in May so we'll be gone as soon as school is out."

He turned all the way to face her. "Really? You never intended to stay here?"

She nodded.

He put his hands on his hips. "So we're doing all this," he waved a hand, taking in the shabby waiting room and the corridor with the conference room. "This whole thing with Tim and Allie and you're not even going to be here in a few months?"

She blinked, taken aback by how quickly he'd gotten upset and how mad he was.

"I don't know why our plans for residency have anything to do with Allie beating Tim up."

"The issue isn't your plans, it's that Allie and I are investing in this process because you demanded it, and you and Tim aren't risking anything."

"I didn't demand this, the league did."

"Oh, that's right. You wanted to call the cops."

She stood to face him, putting her tall boots to work to try to get some control back. "I'm sorry Allie is so upset, but we had to take action if they were going to be on the team together."

"Why in the hell does Tim even need to be on the team? He could have quit. Hockey's Allie's whole existence, and now she's on freaking probation because your kid has some kind of whim to try a new sport. For all you know, the next place you live won't even have hockey."

"The league is open for anyone to play—no one said Tim had to have experience."

"I'm not talking about whether the kid can score a goal, Clare. Mediation isn't a game for Allie. She's been having a rough time and this crap with Tim has made it rougher." He walked away from her, his long legs covering the length of the small room in two angry strides. "You couldn't have missed Mary's revelation she's not in with the girls in her class—her own cousin didn't invite her to that sleepover. So I told her mediation would help. Since she and Tim both like hockey, at the end of this, they could wind up friends. She said okay. She agreed to try even though…well…you saw her." He raised his shoulders and let them drop. "So now I feel like an idiot because the last thing she should be doing is making friends with someone who's leaving. I'm trying to help her build a base she can count on."

He seemed to have calmed down so she pulled her anger back, too. She hoped the kids hadn't heard them.

"He's going to be here for the entire school year."

"The school year is over in six months, Clare. What's the point of a six-month friendship?"

Lila stuck her head out of the conference room. "We're ready for you."

Clare hesitated. She wanted to explain to Bryan that it wasn't a waste of time for Allie to get to know Tim. They had met a lot of interesting people in different places, but looking at it from his perspective, she had a harder time justifying the idea.

He brushed past her and went down the hall. Lila ducked back inside the room. Bryan waited in the doorway, one arm holding the door open for her, the same way Tim had waited for Allie.

She wished he hadn't done that. If he'd been some other guy or they hadn't been fighting, she might have appreciated that small, respectful gesture, but she had to pass much too close to him. She turned her shoulder away but she couldn't avoid the pinpricks of nerves that jumped as she passed him. She felt as if the cashmere sweater was standing up with static charge.

It's been too long, Clare. That's all this physical awareness means. It's not Bryan in particular, it would happen with any man.

She pulled her arms in close, rubbing the skin to bring her attention back to the conference room. She wished she'd reversed her outfit, because her take-charge boots and don't-mess-with-me jeans would be hidden under the table. Tim looked happy, at least. If anything it was Allie, hunched inside her red Twin Falls Cowboys hoodie, who looked as uncomfortable as Clare felt.

The girl didn't look up, not when Clare sat next to Tim and not when Bryan, still frowning, took the last seat at the circular table between his daughter and Lila.

The mediator, who was older than Clare, probably close to sixty, had her silvery hair pulled back into a bun and her glasses hanging from a beaded chain. Clare had time to notice a sophisticated sound-and-video system in one corner before Lila pushed a stack of papers across the table toward her.

"As you know, we're here, all of us together, to help Allie and Tim find ground where they're both comfortable standing. They might not come out of this process friends, but that's not the goal."

Clare glanced at Bryan but he kept his gaze on Lila.

The mediator continued, "Our goal is to reduce the tension in their encounters so they can continue to go to school together and play on their team together. I can say definitively that they're going to learn a lot about themselves and each other as we go."

She gestured to the papers she'd put in front of Clare and Bryan.

"This is the mediation agreement. Both kids signed it in their individual sessions and now you parents can read it through and sign it if you'll be able to support the kids in these steps."

Bryan picked up his pen and flipped the page over, obviously ready to sign.

"I love your enthusiasm, Mr. James, but please read

the plan before you sign. You'll be here with Allie and it's important you know what you're agreeing to—not everyone wants to go forward after they see the commitment."

He put his pen down. "Absolutely. We all need to be committed, that's for sure."

Clare ignored the comment even though she was sure it was directed at her and started scanning her pages. The first one looked like boilerplate stuff, laying out the mediation guidelines. The second consisted of points Allie and Tim must have worked out with Lila. They were going to meet once a week for six weeks—

"Six weeks!" Bryan said. "That's..."

When he realized they were all looking at him, he lowered his voice. "I don't...I mean...what takes so long?"

Clare wouldn't have put it that way, might not have even said anything, but she was certainly interested in the answer. Six weeks of enforced proximity to Allie and Bryan seemed more like penance than mediation.

"Relationships take time. People don't change overnight. Six weeks gives us time to work on the surface issues and uncover whatever the root causes may be."

Bryan pushed the paper away from him. She wasn't sure he was aware he'd done it, but she knew he was considering walking out. Clare tightened her grip on her pen. She hoped he wasn't going to mention that she and Tim were leaving. The last thing she wanted was to fight with Tim in front of Bryan and Allie and she knew he would be all over any hint of support for his arguments.

"Are you sure you're okay with all this, Allie?" Bryan half whispered.

His daughter crossed her arms and hunched down in her chair. She looked younger than thirteen. "Didn't you say I have to?"

"Maybe we…" He looked at each of them, rolling his pen back and forth between his fingers, and then pulled the papers in again. "Yeah. You do."

"We do," Lila said.

"Right." Bryan went back to reading the agreement, Clare continued with her own. Six weeks of meetings during which the kids would also perform community service to make reparations for the damage to the rink.

Danny, apparently, had a storage space he wanted cleaned out and remade into a party room. When she reached the bottom of the second page, she saw that the kids had already signed. Tim's signature was a messy scrawl, familiar to her from countless school papers over the years. Allie's name was carefully scripted in fussy, looping cursive with a cheerful smiley face dotting the *i* that was much more girly than anything she'd have expected from the Cowboys' star center.

Clare bumped Tim's forearm with her elbow and raised her eyebrows, pen poised over the line for her signature. He made an impatient gesture with his hand for her to go ahead. She wondered how often the victim was the most enthusiastic participant in mediation.

She signed.

Bryan pushed his packet toward her and she pushed hers across the table for him. His signature was bold, each letter clear and dark. She noticed that his middle initial was an *X* and she wondered what it stood for. Clare smoothed her hand over the paper and looked up to see him watching her. He was leaning forward slightly with his hands flat on the table in front of him.

Once she signed, they'd be in it together. Tim and Allie would get to know each other and inevitably she and Bryan would, as well.

She could back out now. Sure, Tim would be miserable, but as everyone kept pointing out, they were only going to be here for six months. When they got settled someplace new, he'd forget about Twin Falls and Allie, maybe even about hockey.

She hesitated, her pen resting on the page. Next to her Tim fidgeted, giving his hair that flick he'd been practicing to make it lie exactly right across his forehead. She got another whiff of his new scent. Across the table, Allie was slouching, her arms still folded, her long, dark braid with the frayed-looking ends lying on her shoulder, a perfect picture of misery. Lila smiled serenely, but then, she was getting paid to be serene, wasn't she? Bryan hadn't moved.

Clare sighed. She didn't really have a choice. The four of them were already wound up in each other and that wouldn't change until she and Tim left. She signed her name and capped the pen. That was it. For better or worse.

CHAPTER SEVEN

"So I'd like to get a few things straight."

Clare picked up a stack of books and put it onto the top shelf of the bookcase in the family room. Tim was behind her, lying on his stomach across the beanbag chair, playing his Xbox. If he'd been younger, she'd have sat him down at the dining room table for this conversation, but being a teenager had made him allergic to eye contact. Shuffling around and conducting sideways conversations left her slightly off balance, but if she came at him directly, he'd clam up.

"Uh-huh." He twisted his body, in tune with the action on the screen. In contrast, she was going to have to come back later and put the books in order because it was all she could manage to keep mechanically stuffing them on the shelves. Pretending to ignore him was harder than it looked.

"I'm going along with mediation and you can stay on the hockey team." She shoved another stack of books onto the shelf and realized they were backward, spine in. She started flipping them around. "For now."

He kept his eyes on the game but shifted so he was sitting up. She'd caught his attention. "But?"

"But, the minute you and Allie have another speck of trouble, you have to tell me."

"Mom, I'm—"

"I know. You're handling it." She dropped a paperback but ignored it. If she bent to pick it up, she might accidentally make eye contact and then she'd have to wait to ambush him again some other time. "But bullying and fighting are not things for you to handle alone. You could be hurt here, Tim, seriously hurt."

"By Allie?"

"Yes, by Allie!" Her curly cursive signature might have been all girl, but the sound of Tim's head hitting the floor wasn't something that could be erased by smiley-face-dotted *i*'s.

"It's not like that."

She turned to face him, oblique conversations be damned. "Well, what is it like?"

"Mom. Please."

"What?" Bryan had said she was on the outs with the girls at school, girls who were writing poems about Tim. "Is Allie jealous?"

"Jealous of what?"

"Of you. Because the girls like you."

"No." Tim spun away from her. "I don't want to talk about Allie with you."

"You don't have a choice."

"Ugh. Mom. She doesn't like me. She's not jealous of those girls. What else can you possibly want me to explain?"

"Why she hit you."

"Because..." Tim faced her again. She recognized his expression. Contrition. "I said something to her that I shouldn't have. Nothing bad!" He held up both hands. "I swear. Nothing I thought was bad. She misunderstood." He paused. "Or I misunderstood her. I swear it was mostly because I didn't know her, which I do now. Sort of."

"I'm not following you."

"Why do you have to understand? We're working it out."

"You're my son, Tim. I'm in charge. I can't have you in dangerous situations on your own."

Tim tossed the controller into the basket next to the couch and grabbed his boots. "What you mean is that you can't let me have my own life or make my own friends. It's bad enough you drag me around everywhere like…like that box of books. Can't you butt out now that we're here?"

"Letting you have your privacy and ignoring a potentially dangerous situation are two different things."

"Maybe you're the one…" He stopped himself, cramming his foot into his boot and jerking the laces hard. "Forget it."

"No, Tim. I want to know what you're thinking."

"No."

"'I'm the one' what? What were you going to say?"

"You're the one who's jealous."

"What?"

"You're jealous because I'm making friends and you're not. You don't want to stay anywhere because you know you won't make friends and I will. You always said I could talk to you about anything. Well, I keep telling you that I don't want to move anymore and you keep ignoring me. Why are you afraid to even test it out?"

A piece of crumpled newsprint settling in the box near her feet was the only sound in the room. The silence between them stretched, thick and uncomfortable, until he bent his head to tug his other boot on. She jumped down from the stool and walked over to him.

He stood up and she wondered if he'd let her hug him, but he put his hands in the pockets of his baggy jeans.

"Tim, I'm sorry this is hard for you to understand. I'm not doing it to hurt you or to make you miserable."

"But I am miserable. What's the difference if you're doing it on purpose or not?"

"You know the difference. We move for my work, not to purposely hurt you."

"Other people have jobs like yours and they don't move all the time. Couldn't you get a job where Lindsey works in Seattle?"

"So you want to move to Seattle?"

"No! I don't want to move anywhere, but you're always saying it's hard to get jobs and we're lucky you have this one. Maybe Lindsey could help you get a regular job and we could stay there."

She hesitated, not sure what to say, but he interpreted her silence as a rebuke.

"Forget it. You're not going to change. But, while we're here, you gotta ease up," he said. "Please."

He grabbed his jacket from the floor where he'd dropped it when he came in and went out the front door. She wanted to call after him to zip his coat and to wear a hat and what time would he be back.

She sat down on the stool.

Her cell phone was in her pocket. She reached for it and called Lindsey. Her hands were shaking so she needed two tries to put the call through.

"Hey, girlfriend," Lindsey said. "How's the hockey dad treating you?"

She swallowed.

"Lindsey…"

"Clare? What's wrong?"

"Tim and I had another fight."

"Is it the girl again?"

"No. It's me." Her voice cracked on the last word. She gripped the phone harder.

"Tell me what happened."

What happened? She wasn't even sure. A book she'd stood on the shelf suddenly fell over landing on the wood floor with a bang, startling her. She stood up and walked up the four shallow steps into the kitchen.

"It's the same argument. He wants to stay here. But he was so mad and he left before we resolved anything. Lindsey, it's…oh, God, Lindsey…I keep thinking about Gretchen. I mean, Tim's right here with me but I can see the future and he's going to be gone."

"He won't be gone," Lindsey said. "He's just growing up. Your family will change, but you'll still have him."

Clare took a glass out of the cupboard and ran water from the tap. She took a sip but it made her stomach queasy. She looked out the window at the snow in the backyard that had turned dirty and gray after partially melting on the warm day.

"I don't mean that. I mean, he's so mad at me. If I don't figure this out, his anger will get worse and worse until he leaves. It isn't an argument that'll blow over."

"Okay. You have time, though. You can work on a solution."

"He said I'm scared. And I am. He's right. I'm so scared, Linds."

"Scared of what?"

"When Gretchen died, I couldn't see how I was going

to make it. Everything I saw or touched or felt hurt because of her." She paused, the pain still strong even after twenty years. Her whole world had been Gretchen and when her sister was gone, Clare had stopped caring. She'd run wild, partying at school, hooking up with guys, taking risks, looking for something to stop the hurt. "I was so mad at myself when I got pregnant because I was sure I wouldn't be able to love him."

"I remember. I remember the day he was born and I saw you holding him and it was the first time in so long that I was sure you were going to be okay. You came back for him. You loved him, Clare. You never hesitated."

"I had a fight with Bryan, too. He found out we're moving and he said, in so many words, that Allie shouldn't waste her time getting to know Tim."

"Way to get on board with the mediation. No wonder his kid is a bully."

"No." Clare turned her back on the window, leaning against the sink, alone in the kitchen of this house where she still didn't feel at home. "He's trying to take care of his daughter. She's having trouble socially as it is. If I were in his place, I'd probably feel the same."

"All right." Lindsey paused. "I'm sense there's a 'but' coming."

"But it sucks that he sees Tim that way. And that's my fault. All this time, I believed I was giving him this cool gift, meeting new people and having new experiences. Maybe it was cool for a while, but what he wants now is to put down roots. He wants to matter. It's that peer thing—when he was little, I was enough for him, but now he wants to find people outside his family. It's normal and healthy."

"And?"

"I don't know if I can give him what he wants," she whispered. "After Gretchen and my mom, I put myself back together for Tim. I made myself start loving again. I've got you and my dad and Tim and that's all I can handle. I'm not sure I'm strong enough to open up to anyone else. More people means more chance something can go wrong. If we stay here or anywhere, I'm going to start caring for people. I won't be able to help it. I don't know if I can risk that, not even for Tim."

"It might not be only for him, Clare. You—" Lindsey's voice shook and Clare heard her friend's tears. "You were a little girl and you watched Gretchen die. You lived through something that would have crushed other people. It *did* crush your mom and your dad. But it didn't crush you. You are strong enough, Clare. Right now. Every day that you spend with Tim, that you love him. Every day that you're my best friend. Every day, you're strong enough."

"I don't feel strong enough."

"Oh, Clare."

"He's going to start to hate me," she said.

The silence told Clare everything. When Lindsey recovered and said, "You're doing your best," the words were too little too late.

Tim was going to learn to hate her if she couldn't figure out how to put her fears behind her and let people into their lives. Tim had never lost anyone he cared about. He had no idea what it meant to have to go on when someone you loved was gone. He wanted a community, someplace he belonged, but he had no idea how much caring could hurt.

DESPITE THE FREEZING temperature, he'd taken the phone onto the small balcony off the living room because he didn't want Allie to overhear him making this call.

It wasn't going well.

He'd made his pitch, but as soon as Erin started talking, he knew she was going to say no. He could hear it in the way she said his name as if he was a five-year-old who'd asked one too many times for a Happy Meal. He hated when she said his name like that.

"Bryan, I can't listen to the guilt trip anymore. We agreed that I was going to take this once-in-a-lifetime opportunity." She stressed the words, making it sound as if he didn't put enough value on her new career. "But practically since the second I left you've been bugging me to come back."

"We were fine until she started fighting." He thought that was true. On the other hand, there must be some reason for the fighting—it wasn't as though she woke up one day and started punching people for no reason, so there must have been something going on that he'd missed. "She won't talk to me."

"She's thirteen, Bryan. She doesn't talk to me, either."

"You haven't seen her. This isn't normal teenage stuff. She's upset. The divorce was bad enough, but maybe all this change is too hard on her."

"On Allie or on you?"

"On her. She needs you."

"You can't do this to me, Bryan," Erin said. "We were too young when we got married, way too young when we got pregnant. I gave everything up to take care of Allie. Is it fair to ask me to quit the tour, the first real thing I've ever done for myself, just because you can't figure out how to talk to your own daughter?"

Bryan shivered. He was wearing a pullover warm-up jacket that wasn't nearly thick enough for the cold night.

"Erin, please," he said. "This can't wait for the tour to be over."

"I can't quit in the middle."

"You won't."

"Don't argue with me about words. Can't, won't, what difference does it make?" He heard the impatience in her voice that meant she was about to blow up at him. This was how so many of their fights went—they hadn't been able to listen to each other for so many years, he almost couldn't remember a time when they'd been friends.

"No difference, because either way I don't know what I'm doing and she's the one getting hurt."

"You had thirteen years to figure out what you were doing, but you were always gone. Work and work and more work. You let me take care of everything and, I'm sorry, Bryan, but you have to figure this out now."

He paced forward and leaned on his elbows on the wooden railing. He wouldn't deny that he'd been gone. When he took the sales job, they were desperate for the money and without a college degree he hadn't had a lot of options. Dutton Skates had been willing to take him because he had enough of a hockey rep to get people to talk to him. And then it turned out he was actually good at sales.

He'd always planned to cut back. He'd wanted to be home more, to show up for dinner every night and attend every school play and have the kind of family he'd seen, but never been a part of.

"I wouldn't have been gone so much if I hadn't felt like I was intruding when I was home."

"Not this again."

"Yes, this again. You never let me be a dad. When I fed her you said I let too much air in with the bottles. You used to take her diapers off and redo them when I changed her. You were happier when I was gone."

"I couldn't have forced you out of the house if you'd really wanted to be there."

"You thought you were going to be an NHL wife and you never forgave me when I didn't come through."

"You never forgave yourself. Every time you told yourself you were making money to make things up to me and Allie, you were trying to make yourself feel better."

"I wish you'd mentioned this willingness to live in poverty earlier, because despite what you think, I wanted to be here more."

"Well, you're there now. You're having your chance at it, and you're complaining."

"I'm asking you for help, not complaining. She seems so lost." *And angry.*

He wondered what Clare would be doing differently if Allie were her daughter. He could imagine Clare giving Allie that look, the one she'd given him the night of the fight that had made him so ashamed. Not that Allie had anything to be ashamed about. He bet Clare had other looks, useful looks that would help a person set his daughter straight.

"I'll call her, Bryan. I'll try to get her to tell me what's going on, but she doesn't talk to me. I'll check the tour schedule. As soon as we have any kind of break, I'll fly home. But you have to stop asking me to quit. I should be allowed to take this time for me. I should be able to count on you. Allie should be able to count on you."

"Fine," Bryan said, his voice laced with frustration and anger. "I'll take care of her, but not because I want it that way."

Bryan clicked his phone shut. The vertical blinds rattled and he knew, knew before he spun around and saw her, that she was there. Allie, her face white and her eyes big, was standing in the doorway, the blinds framing her in the space where the light from the living room met the dark of the night. She looked starkly alone. One fist was pushed tight against her mouth and he heard a stifled sob.

"Oh, Allie. No."

"I'm sorry," she whispered. She backed up three steps before turning and running through the living room and down the hall to her room.

"Allie," he said. He went after her but she'd locked her door. It was a flimsy button lock on the cheap, hollow core door. He could have broken it if that wouldn't have freaked her out entirely. He knocked, tapping his fist against the poster of the Buffalo Sabres she'd taped up. "Honey. You have to let me in."

Silence.

"What you heard," he said. "It's not what it sounded like. Please open the door."

Allie's music switched on inside. He thought she'd closed herself off, but then he heard her behind the door. If he was right, the sound he'd heard was the slick whisper of her jersey as she slid down the door to sit on the floor. Bryan leaned his head against the wood. A shadow blocked the light under the door. She was there, he was sure of it.

"I called your mom, Allie. I..." He closed his eyes but then opened them again. "I suppose the parenting experts would say I shouldn't admit that I'm in over my head to you, but you're smart enough that you already know it." He paused, and then sat down. He made enough noise so she couldn't miss what he was doing. He moved his hand carefully so it lined up exactly with the edge of the shadow on the floor on the other side of the door.

"When your mom told me she was going on the tour with Lush, I worried she was going to move you to California. She says this tour is once-in-a-lifetime, but you know how she is. If she decides L.A is what she wants, she's going to find a way to stay out there."

He couldn't help smiling. Erin was a force of nature when she made her mind up about something.

"Anyway, the thing I thought...the only thing...was that I couldn't let her take you. If she'd tried to take you, I was going to fight her. So when you stayed here with me, it was what I wanted. But now, with everything that's happened, you seem so sad all the time. Maybe what I was doing, keeping you here, was selfish. It's what I want. But is it what's best for you? You need...God...I don't even know what. I want to do this right...help you get through whatever it is that's got you all banged up. I...I'm asking for some help, baby."

He wished she'd answer him, but she was silent.

"It's you and me, Allie. We have to make this work."

He leaned his head against the door and waited. He wasn't leaving first, not if there was a chance she was still there. He heard her moving, standing up, and he thought that was it. But then he heard her whisper,

"Good night, Dad." The light flicked off and the music cut off abruptly. She'd plugged in her headphones.

He stayed on the floor for a long time, his knee gradually cramping to the point that he was going to be paying for it for a week at least. He couldn't make himself move away, though. She'd reached out to him. *Three words.* It was enough. It had to be enough. For tonight at least.

BRYAN WATCHED INTENTLY as Allie skated backward, her stick sweeping the ice as she played defense against a kid who clearly had no idea how to defend against the poke check she'd perfected in third grade. She took the puck away and headed back down the ice but when she dumped it to Cody, the left wing on her line, he missed the pass and lost it again. Allie smacked her stick on the ice in frustration.

With one eye on the game, he looked to Clare, sitting three rows above him. Her attention was right where it had been the whole game, on the book in her lap. Tim had played a shift at the beginning of this period and she hadn't even looked up for that.

Allie shot, but the goalie blocked it. He and Allie got tangled up and the puck lay on the ice, uncovered, a big fat gift for the Cowboys. Cody and the other wing were so busy getting out of the way they didn't see the puck before one of the defensemen on the other team gave it a long hard shot toward the other end of the ice. Allie yelled at Cody, pointing at the net.

Bryan winced and blew on his hands. It was going to be a long year.

Correction, it was going to be a long four months until hockey season ended. Six months until Clare and Tim packed up and left for parts unknown. In the meantime, he was supposed to make sure his daughter connected with Tim so she could get her mediation certificate. He shook his head at the utter circular stupidity of the plan, but then, it had never been his plan in the first place. His job was to make sure the mediation worked, not to question why they were bothering. After the way he'd hurt Allie the other night with his comment to Erin, he was determined to do a better job.

It would probably be a step in the right direction if he could get Clare to sit with the other team parents.

He climbed the three rows of bleachers to sit in front of her. She didn't notice. She was wearing that same belted coat from the other night. It accentuated her trim waist and the flare of her hips. Her dark denim jeans were a lot more sophisticated than the Wrangler jeans he was used to seeing on his sister, and her boots had heels, setting them years away from the functional winter foot-gear most of the rest of the spectators were wearing.

In all his years watching Allie play hockey, Bryan had never once noticed how good another player's mom looked in her jeans. He'd never wondered how hard it would be to get a player's mom out of her jeans and into a skirt or even into nothing at all. Hockey mom and sex had never been a connection Bryan made. Not until Clare. Now he couldn't be near her for five minutes before his thoughts started down paths they hadn't taken since before he married Erin.

He looked back at the action on the ice. He was not, under any circumstances, going to let himself think about Clare that way again.

If she ever found out he was having dirty daydreams about her, she'd probably run screaming, anyway.

On the other hand, he was positive she'd been

checking him out that night at the gym. She was only going to be here for six months. Maybe she'd like a fling. The word *fling* was like a cold shower. He and Erin had started out on a giddy rush—they'd been young and horny and every second they spent together was exciting. He'd mistaken that physical connection for love and by the time he realized his mistake, he'd been married and Allie was on the way.

For most of his marriage he'd been nothing more than Erin's paycheck.

Nope. His body might be waking back up to the potential in other women—and Clare was hard to resist— but if he did decide to get involved with someone, this time he was going to be sure it was about more than sex. He wasn't going to take any steps to address what his body felt for Clare.

No matter how much he wanted to.

He sighed. Tried to stay positive. Allie's team sucked but at least she was still allowed to play. He could do his part to make sure that didn't change. If community mediation meant building bridges in a hands-off, no-kissing-no-matter-how-sexy-a-person-was way, well, he'd manage. It was only six weeks. Or six months. Whichever deadline you picked, one way or the other, Clare was leaving and when she did, he was sure he would stop obsessing about sex with hockey moms.

"Hi, Clare," he said. Brilliant cover. She'd never guess he was considering crossing the line from mediation partner to lover if he kept up this level of inspired conversation.

"Bryan," she answered. She didn't sound any more comfortable than he was.

"Tim's a good skater for a kid who never played before."

"He did a lot of figure skating the last place we lived."

"Figure skating?" She gave him that sharp look, and he quickly changed his mind about making a figure-skating joke. "Guess it paid off."

"You could say that."

"Where did you live before this?"

"Baltimore."

"Whoa. Baltimore to Twin Falls. That's a switch," Bryan said. "No wonder the girls are into Tim—he's probably the only kid they know who's lived in a city that big."

"Yes, we have an interesting life."

She wasn't giving him a single thing to work with and he was almost out of small talk. He tried again. "Your job keeps you moving."

She pushed a strand of hair behind her ear. "I'd rather not talk about this, if it's okay with you."

He shrugged and went back to watching the game. Allie was on the bench and the second line was having trouble with the center from the other team. Maybe Clare would feel more a part of things at the games if she knew what was going on. Bryan pointed to the center, his eyes never leaving the kid's back as he followed the action.

"Number 4 is the only threat on their team. He's taken every shot so far. If they shut him down, the scoring stops."

She put her finger between the pages of her book to mark her place and looked where he was pointing, but he could tell because her eyes weren't tracking the play that she had no idea what he'd said.

"Number four on the other team. White helmet. Moves smooth enough to switch to figure skating if he wants to."

She zeroed in on the kid, a hint of a smile tipping the corners of her mouth up. "Got him."

"He's the only one who shoots. If we could cut him off, their offense would fall apart."

"I'm sure Tim will try his best."

"His best?"

"With the shutting down. Stopping number four?"

"Tim plays offense."

"Oh." She lifted the book and shrugged. "That's why I stick with this."

"You want me to run through the rules for you? Hockey's not that complicated."

"Nope. Hockey is Tim's thing."

She opened the book again. He was staring so he forced his attention back to the ice, but he couldn't help himself. He kept glancing over to check but she was absorbed in the book. She hadn't been kidding around. She wasn't having trouble getting involved with the hockey team, she wasn't interested.

Tim went back out for another shift and he managed to get his stick on a rebound. His swing didn't have any power behind it so the shot didn't go anywhere, but still, it was good to see him connecting and getting the idea. Clare didn't notice. She wasn't even aware her son was on the ice.

"You're really not going to watch?"

"Really not."

He thought he saw her smiling.

"But…" He stopped.

She closed the book, sliding it into the leather bag at her side and putting her hands on her knees.

"What, Bryan?"

He had her full attention and he wondered what exactly he'd started. He wasn't sure he wanted her thinking about him with the intelligence that was so obvious in her eyes. What would a person like her see if she got a good look at him?

But then, even though he hadn't meant to, he started talking. "It's just…" *Yep.* He was going to embarrass himself in front of her again. He had to. He was sitting next to this person who seemed to know what she was doing with her kid. Maybe she could help him figure out his. "It feels like all Allie and I can talk about is hockey. If I didn't watch her games, what would we have left?"

"The other stuff in her life."

Other stuff? Bryan tilted his head. What kind of answer was that? He felt as awkward and out of step as he had the other night when she and Mary were joking about their kids and their crushes when his kid was sitting home alone. He'd put himself out there, let Clare have another peek at the underbelly of his anxiety and she gave him a flip answer? Like she and Tim had so much they shared that she could just skip whole big parts of it because there was all that "other stuff" waiting for them. They probably talked about Shakespeare at the dinner table. Or figure-skating moves. Or what it felt like to have girls following you around writing poetry about you.

He was getting tired of feeling dumb in front of her.

"I guess with all the other stuff you enjoy together, you and Tim don't talk about hockey."

Clare seemed to remember she had a kid on the ice and she squinted at the action, scanning until she found Tim.

"It's always been just the two of us. We're close."

"Close? What does that mean? He tells you about school and his friends, or you play Monopoly every Saturday, or you read each other's diaries, or what?"

"We..." she hesitated. "Yes."

"Yes? Yes, what?"

"Yes, we talk about lots of things," she said, sounding as irritated and impatient as he felt. "Tim and I are very close." She didn't look at him, just reached down, pulling her book out and opening it quickly.

He had no idea what had happened. She was upset, obviously. Trying to tune him out, definitely. But why?

SHE HAD HOPED SHE would like being in the stands. Even if she didn't watch the game because the banging and the falling and the smashing into the sides made her nervous, she was here, where Tim could see her, being supportive. Freezing to death, but not complaining. Being a hockey mom.

She'd seen Bryan when she first came in, but he was sitting with a crowd of other parents and she hadn't known how to approach them.

Hi, I'm Clare Sampson. You might have heard that my son was beaten up in the lobby of this very rink?

Hi, I understand your child's team lost the game last weekend because Allie was benched for hitting another child. Guess what? That's my son!

Or even better...*Hi, my name is Clare and if I decide*

the mediation isn't working, your superstar ticket to the play-offs is out the door.

Yeah. She didn't guess she'd be so welcome there with the other parents. But then Bryan came up to sit with her and she'd been relieved. Tim was right the other night when he said she was having trouble meeting people. It wasn't only that she couldn't muster the energy—even when she did try, she was running into trouble. Part of the issue was Twin Falls. It was a small town and most of the people she met had grown up here—none of them needed any new friends. The tech group at the bank were all young, single and more likely to have interests in common with Tim than with her.

The details had changed since the last time they'd moved, too. In the past, she'd been able to jump into mom conversations and connect with other women over universal problems like potty training or sleep or how to navigate the world of parent-teacher conferences. With a middle schooler, though, the mom conversations revolved around social issues and she didn't know enough about any of the kids to really get involved. For the first time in a long time, Clare was lonely. She'd been grateful that Bryan made the effort.

There'd been a moment when he'd sat down in front of her that she'd wondered again what it would feel like to push her fingers through his thick, unruly hair. The unfairness of this situation was overwhelming. Not only was Tim being bullied by a girl who wasn't quite as tall as he was, Clare was having fantasies about the girl's father and his gorgeous, thick hair.

For a person who'd always prided herself on keeping her date separate from her son, this was crossing a lot of lines.

Good thing her fantasies about Bryan evaporated every time they had a conversation.

When he'd started quizzing her about her relationship with Tim, she'd wished he'd stayed where he'd been, three rows down. Too far away to admire his hair properly, but also too far for him to have asked her that stupid question.

What did she and Tim do together?

Not a whole heck of a lot anymore.

She couldn't say that to Bryan, though. Saying it out loud would make it seem real.

It was useless to try to read. She was so irritated the words were running together on the page. She slammed her book shut.

"We do a lot of things together. Camping..."

"In the winter?"

"We like museums."

"In Twin Falls?"

"Well, no. You didn't ask what we did together yesterday."

"I'm asking now. Tell me about yesterday."

Tim had slept until eleven o'clock and then left the house with his backpack. He'd turned up for dinner but she'd been on a conference call for work so he'd eaten by himself in front of the TV.

"I don't see the point, Bryan. You and Allie are not me and Tim."

She hadn't meant to hurt him, but she suspected she had. She wasn't even sure how, but the way he tucked his chin in and nodded reminded her of Allie the night of that first fight.

"No," he said slowly. "No, we're not."

HE STAYED ON the bleachers in front of her because damn if he was going to let her chase him away with her judgmental remarks. He didn't turn around again, though, not even to let her know when Tim tipped the puck in at the end of the third period. The Cowboys swarmed him, thumping his helmet and slapping his shoulder pads. Bryan was positive the kid hadn't even known the puck was coming at him; scoring the goal by deflection more than intent. But the quick fist pump Tim made afterward didn't look any less joyous than if he'd squared up and shot on purpose. Allie didn't join in the celebration. She leaned on her stick, her head so low she blended right in with the players on the other team.

That wasn't like her. Not at all. She was tough and competitive and had never been a graceful loser, not even when she was four and the games were played cross-ice and only lasted ten minutes. Heck, not even when she was four and the game was Candy Land at home on the dining room table.

She'd always been generous with her teammates, though. Passed when she should. Didn't showboat after goals. What he was seeing now was a kind of pouting resentment that concerned him. Another kid with another coach might even get benched for that kind of behavior.

Well, tonight when they talked about hockey, because he was damned if he could find one other thing she'd respond to, he was going to make sure he brought this attitude up. Allie might be stuck with an inexperienced dad, but she came by her competitive tendencies honestly—he could explain to her about what it meant to be a leader on a team.

Tim skated over to Allie who dropped her stick on

purpose to avoid having to talk to him. He looked up toward his mom's spot in the bleachers. Bryan clapped and the kid waved. Bryan relented, turning around to congratulate Clare. She was reading again. She'd missed her son's first goal. When he looked back to the ice, Tim was on his way to the bench. He must have known his mom wasn't going to lift her head.

Clare could pretend all she wanted, but Bryan would bet that all was not perfect in the Sampson house, either.

AFTER THE GAME HE WAITED for Allie in the hallway outside the locker room. A bunch of other parents were milling around, rehashing the game, complimenting one another's kids and picking apart the penalties against the other team. Two boys, little brothers, played keep-away with a tape ball until one of their mothers told them to put the sticks down.

The locker room door opened with a burst of laughter and a knot of boys came out, dragging their gear bags and grabbing sticks out of the rack. Tim was right in the middle of them, his face glowing as one of the other boys slapped him on the back. Bryan stepped back to let them go by, but Tim hesitated, giving him a tentative grin, clearly unsure if the connection between them was going to continue outside the mediation sessions.

No time like the present, he told himself as he gave Tim a thumbs-up. "Nice goal," he said.

Tim's grin came out in full force. "You saw? I wasn't sure you saw."

"Everybody saw, kid."

"My mom missed it. She hates hockey." The kid was

pissed. Clare might believe it was enough to show up, but Tim wasn't buying it.

He hated that he'd tainted Tim's triumph by reminding him that Clare had missed the goal. The other boys were looking at them and even though Bryan was hands-off when it came to kids and hockey, he made an exception to his policy.

The players who came up in the Twin Falls league had all heard the stories about him—he was held up as an ideal by some of the coaches and parents. *Practice hard and you can get drafted like Bryan James.* He never traded on that slice of local celebrity for himself. His memories of his hockey career and his wasted opportunities were different from the town's. But maybe he could use it this once to give Tim a hand fitting in on the team. The more he helped Tim settle in, the better off Allie would be, he hoped.

"Come here," he said, holding out his hand and motioning for Tim's stick. "You don't need any skating tips, but if you're going to score more goals you should work on your stick handling."

The kid handed the stick over and Bryan was aware of the crowd of boys and parents watching. This was why he didn't get involved—too much pressure to be something special when really he was a middle-aged guy who'd been good more than a decade ago. Still, he did know how to play and Tim's skating was good enough that he could be a productive team player if he learned to shoot.

He took Tim's stick and measured it against his body. "This is an inch too long for you. Coach can find someone to help you cut it if your mom doesn't know how. You'll have more control if it's the right size."

Tim nodded.

Bryan took the stick and showed him how to position his hands, not too close together, not too far apart. The boys around him slid their hands down their sticks, taking in the free lesson.

He swung in slow motion, making sure to point out where the stick should hit the ice, six inches behind the puck, and how to finish with the stick pointed at the goalie. "Snap it. It's a quick shot so use your wrists."

He handed the stick back and motioned for Tim to take a swing. The other kids pressed back against the walls to give him room. Tim swung and actually made a decent cut.

"Looks all right," he said. Tim nodded and took another swing. A few of the other boys mimicked his moves.

He didn't realize Allie was behind him until she spoke. Last year she'd started dressing in the bathroom, not the locker room with the boys, so she hadn't been with the team when they came out.

"It wasn't even a shot," she said quietly. "He moved his stick and accidentally bumped the puck."

She dropped the handle of her bag and pushed past the boys who were asking Tim to show them what Bryan had said. None of them spoke to her. They didn't even notice her. Bryan grabbed her bag, lifting it onto his shoulder and taking her stick in his other hand.

When he got close to the lobby, he saw Clare. She was hanging back, watching Tim in the middle of the group of boys. He hadn't noticed her, but she must have seen him take her son aside because she said, "You didn't have to do that."

It wasn't a thank-you and they both knew it. Her

distrust went so deep, that mediator had her work cut out for her. He was already irritated with Allie's bad mood and with himself for letting Clare know more about their issues and with pretty much everything about all of them, and he didn't slow down. "Well, I won't next time."

In fact, he thought, if no one ever mentioned Clare or Tim Sampson to him again, he'd be perfectly happy. He had his hands full with his own family.

CHAPTER EIGHT

"In their session today, Tim and Allie came up with a project plan for the party room."

Clare wasn't really listening. She'd almost called to cancel this mediation session because she was under the gun with the report she had due at work later that month. The language had to be simple enough for the manager to understand but detailed enough to pass the technical-compliance review. She'd gotten as far as dialing Lila's number before she admitted to herself that the real reason she didn't want to come was that she didn't want to see Bryan again. She was struggling with the report, but more than that she was struggling with her physical attraction to the guy.

It hadn't helped her to see him reaching out to Tim after the game. Tim had been on cloud nine on the way home in the car. His coach had told him where to get his stick cut and Tim wouldn't be satisfied until they'd stopped at the hardware store kitty-corner from the diner and asked for Nick. Nick, it turned out, of course, was another hockey fanatic. While he turned on the table saw, measured the stick, cut it and retaped it, Nick regaled Tim with several of his seemingly infinite catalog of Bryan James local-hockey-god stories.

As soon as they got back home, Tim made a beeline for his computer and YouTube. Apparently there were several old college-hockey highlight clips featuring Bryan James. She hadn't watched the videos, but Tim had. She'd heard him playing the same three-minute clip fourteen times before she finally yelled for him to start his homework.

He thought she was irritated that he was on the computer, but she was really mad at herself. When she'd seen Bryan and Tim sharing that lesson after the game, she'd been jealous. Tim's three favorite topics of conversation these days were hockey, Twin Falls and Bryan James. All of those things had converged today and it felt as if Tim was sinking his roots deep into this community against her will. He was making a home for himself and he didn't care if she was part of it.

Late that night, hours after Tim had fallen asleep, she'd looked up the video and watched it. She hadn't been lying when she told Bryan she didn't know anything about hockey, but watching him skate around and sometimes over the defenders in the clips had been thrilling. The speed and wild power she saw in his playing captivated her. She couldn't imagine feeling that strong, that graceful, that good at something as intense as hockey. Then she'd remembered his knee. Getting hurt, even when it meant his career ended, wasn't the same as what happened to her sister, not by any stretch of the imagination, but she guessed Bryan knew a thing or two about loss.

She'd been tempted to look up the details of his injury while she was on the computer. She hadn't done it, though. She'd already imagined how it could have happened, one of those horrid, bone-crushing checks that scared her so badly or maybe even an illegal hit from behind. The truth was, she didn't want to know what had happened. She didn't want to know any more about him than she already did, especially because Lindsey was right. She was interested in Bryan, but her attraction felt different from her usual appreciation of a good-looking, single guy who was fun in bed. She wanted to make Bryan laugh. She wanted to watch him skate. She wanted to see Tim's delight when Bryan gave him a compliment. She wanted to be there when he and Allie finally figured out how to talk to each other and she wanted to get right up close to him and find out what it felt like when he put his arms around her and pulled her in close to his chest.

If she wasn't careful, she could fall for Bryan James. She'd finally find out what it felt like to make love with a guy she wasn't planning to leave.

She had never intended to wonder about that. She had Tim, Lindsey and her dad. They were enough. They had to be enough.

The only way to complete the terms of the mediation was to stay disengaged. Don't connect with Allie. Don't get involved with the project. Definitely don't fantasize about illicit meetings with Mr. Collegiate Hockey 1996.

"Allie, why don't you explain about the collage since it was mostly your idea?" Lila said.

Allie looked at Tim before she started talking and the look wasn't angry. Was it possible the level of her hostility was easing? Clare hoped so. Maybe they'd all be so damn gifted at mediation they could graduate early. Maybe she could also finish her contract early, and she and Tim could shake the snow off their mukluks and find somewhere warm to spend the rest of this godforsaken season.

"Um. Danny wants us to make a party room, which is useful because when I tried to have my birthday at the rink one time, my mom said no because there's no place to eat anything and you can't have cake in the locker room."

That was the longest speech she'd ever heard from Allie. Clare had to agree with Allie's absent mom. She certainly wouldn't eat anything that had come in contact with a hockey locker room, either.

"So I...I mean, Tim and I thought, after we get the room cleaned out...to make it look like a party room more..." She was fumbling around and getting more and more flustered.

Tim broke in. "Allie's got a plan for this collage with all pictures of kids skating and pucks coming at you. She knows this place where you can get stuff printed in 3-D and if we make them different sizes and layer them how she sketched out where some of the pictures stick out, it'll look like you're really in a game."

Allie blushed. "And anyway, Danny says it's fine."

Bryan leaned his arms on the table, watching the interaction between Allie and Tim carefully. He was wearing jeans and a V-neck sweater over a blue-and-white striped shirt with the sleeves pushed back to reveal strong forearms. He had a strip of black leather knotted around the same wrist on which he wore a watch with a black leather band and a rectangular silver face that made her think Art Deco. She wondered about the bracelet. Did it mean something to him or was it just something he wore? She couldn't remember if he'd had it on that night at the gym.

Clare's phone started vibrating in her pocket. She put her hand down, but resisted the urge to pull it out. The meeting wouldn't take much longer and then she could head to work. She wondered if it would be possible to talk the kids out of this collage idea. Cleaning the room out and painting were reasonable, but the collage was going to mean more work and more time.

Lila gestured to Tim who said, "Right. My turn. So the deal with mediation is, we all have to agree. It's consensus, not majority rule. Does this sound okay, Mr. James?"

"You can call me Bryan," he said. "Allie made a sketch for this collage thing?"

Tim nodded.

Bryan turned to face his daughter. "Where did you learn about the 3-D stuff?"

"School. Art class. The Internet."

"You read about art on the Internet?"

At her father's question, Allie's shoulders went up and her chin went down and Clare couldn't remember ever seeing anyone close herself off so fast.

"It seemed like there'd be pictures in a room like that," the girl mumbled. "Danny didn't say we had to."

"I'm not upset or anything, Allie," Bryan said, but then he stopped, and he looked so confused that Clare couldn't help herself. He and Allie were trying so hard to communicate with each other and failing utterly. If she weren't busy being disengaged from the people in the room, she might have felt sorry for them.

"Of course we'll include the 3-D collage," she said in her best efficient, end-of-discussion voice. "This will be the most remarkable party room in Twin Falls."

"It's going to be beast," Tim said.

"I'm in," Bryan said quickly.

Allie's shoulders relaxed. Clare wasn't looking forward to the extra work, but supporting the design had been the right decision.

Lila made a note on a paper in front of her and then said, "Okay, here are the ground rules. You work together, no taking separate shifts. Danny approves the room before I sign off on the certificates. And most important, the project has two foremen. The foremen must be in unanimous agreement about any decision. Consensus is absolutely a requirement for this work. That means if the foremen can't agree on a process or a task, you'll schedule a session with me before you go forward." Lila swept her hand out. "Meet your foremen, Allie James and Tim Sampson."

Allie and Tim?

"The kids are in charge?" Clare blurted.

Lila smiled. "They're the ones making reparations, aren't they?"

"Yes, but..." Clare paused. "Don't you think..."

Tim was watching her. Oh, her boy was smart. He knew exactly how uncomfortable it made her to let him and Allie be in charge of this project and he was waiting for her to open her mouth and step into it. He'd been saying she should back off and let him handle things and here she was, about to prove him right that she was too controlling.

She caught Bryan's eye. He gave a one-shouldered shrug, daring her or commiserating, she couldn't tell. Oh, well, this was the perfect opportunity to show Tim how wrong he was about her. How easygoing she could be. How much he'd wish she was in charge when things got hard.

"Fine," she said, her voice sounding chirpy even to her. "It sounds fun."

Which was a lie. Cleaning out a room full of dirty hockey stuff sounded unappetizing enough. Working under two teenagers, one with a predilection for surliness, the other for chaos, made it worse. Topping it all off, Bryan would be working with her, lifting things and maybe building things and probably wearing a tool belt because men liked tool belts. And he'd be all sexy and strong. All manly and desirable. All off-limits.

She should put in for a transfer to a different mediation group right now. She had a very bad feeling that her intention to stay disengaged was going downhill fast.

"That means you have to do what we say, Mom," Tim said.

"That's the definition of *foremen*."

"Even if what we say isn't what you would say."

"I understand."

"Even if what we say is illogical or insane." He widened his eyes and waggled his fingers under his chin.

"I'm yours to direct."

It was wrong and one of her worst failings as a mother, but somehow, when Tim was at his most mischievous, that was exactly when she loved him a little bit harder.

She'd spent her childhood trying to be good and trying not to upset her parents. Every milestone she passed, growing taller, stronger, closer to being an adult had been mirrored with Gretchen's losses: muscle control, speech and finally her battle to keep living. Any delight Clare had felt in her strength or skill had been tempered by bitter regret over her sister.

When Tim pushed boundaries, her first instinct was always to pull him back. At the same time that she had a hard time giving Tim his freedom, she was fiercely happy that he demanded it. His mischief, stubbornness

and insistence on independence were irrefutable signs
that she had managed to give him a different childhood
from hers. Even when Tim was driving people nuts, even
when his behavior was *bad,* that traitor inside her was
chanting go, go, go.

"Maybe she should call you sir," Allie said quietly.
Clare didn't know her well enough to tell if that was a
dig at her or at Tim or if she was trying to get in on the
joke.

"Allie," Bryan rebuked her, obviously falling into the
"it was a dig" camp, but Tim jumped in.

"Captain," he said.

"Your Highness," Allie added. That time Clare definitely saw a hint of mischief when Allie peeked at Tim
from under her hair.

Maybe Allie wasn't the kid she'd have picked for
Tim to befriend. Okay, she was definitely not that kid.
But he'd never let her pick his friends, not since he was
three and insisted on adopting Carter, the unrepentant
preschool-class nudist. She'd learned to let him go, and
to find the things that were admirable in the kids he
picked no matter how hard she had to look.

"As long as I don't have to call you Lord Supreme
Commander," she said.

Lila opened her calendar. "So, when can you
start?"

OUTSIDE THE BUILDING, Clare caught up to Bryan. "Can
I talk to you for a minute in private?"

Bryan called to Allie on her way to the car and tossed
her the keys. He told her she could turn it on and listen
to the radio. Clare asked Tim to wait in their car, but he

ran after Allie and climbed into the backseat of Bryan's Lexus. She frowned.

"Is it safe to let them turn the car on?"

Bryan laughed. "You worried Allie's going to take it for a joyride?"

"Tim might."

"Really?"

She shrugged. "Probably not. It's your car and he wouldn't want you mad at him." She tugged her scarf down and tucked it into the collar of her coat in a futile effort to block the wind. "That's actually what I wanted to ask you about."

"About my car?"

"About Tim."

The worry line appeared between his eyes. "What about him?"

"He's worked himself up into a serious case of hero worship. You've probably noticed that."

Bryan shrugged. "He seems like a nice kid."

He didn't address the hero-worship comment and she liked him a little more for his obvious discomfort with the subject. This conversation would be easier if he were an egotistical jerk, but she was glad he wasn't.

"I really appreciate that you're being kind to him. He was thrilled with the impromptu lesson after the game yesterday and…well…you can see that he's responding to you."

He didn't say anything, but he stuck his hands in his pockets and didn't quite meet her eyes. She was embarrassing him. She wished he would stop being so appealing.

"But we're leaving, Bryan. My contract is going to end and there's no chance of an extension. Tim is already having a hard time with this and the more you reach out to him, the worse it's going to be when we go."

"So you're asking me to…what?"

Bryan felt irritated. It took everything he had to keep his voice even. First she told him that Tim liked him and that she appreciated that he'd helped her kid and in the next breath she was telling him to back off?

"Don't single him out. Treat him like any other kid," Clare said.

"If you hadn't forced us into mediation with your freak-out about Allie, I might never have talked to your son, right?"

"My freak-out?" Clare said. "They rolled each other through broken glass, Bryan. You weren't there, but if you had been, I'm damn sure you'd have been as horrified as I was."

"The fact remains that this was your idea and now you're trying to set up boundaries." He looked over his shoulder at the car. "Make up your mind, Clare. Should the kids get to know each other or should Allie and I go on our way? You can't make some master list of do's and don'ts and force the rest of us to memorize it."

"I'm not saying that," Clare protested. "I'm asking you to be aware that he's fascinated by you and to try to remember that when he leaves, he's going to be hurt."

Bryan nodded. "That's generally what happens when people leave, you're right about that."

"Stop turning this into a fight, please. I wouldn't expect you to understand."

"Good, because I don't."

"This is my decision, Bryan. You have no right to judge."

"I sure don't know you. You're so sealed up, how

could anyone get close to you? But I can't help wondering why you want to shut us out."

"Well, stop," Clare said. "It doesn't matter if you understand. Just remember that we're leaving. You can skip the hockey-champ thing for Tim. You can save it for the kids who live here."

"Hockey-champ thing?"

"I saw you at the rink. Those kids worship you. Hell, their parents worship you. You took the time to give Tim some pointers and I appreciate it, but no more. It's not necessary to turn him into a hockey fanatic."

"This is ridiculous," Bryan said. "You don't know the first thing about me, either. I can't help the way people around here treat me, but I certainly don't put on any hockey-champ thing. Tim was bummed out because he scored a goal and you weren't watching. I tried to cheer him up. That's all."

Clare looked surprised. "He scored a goal?"

"You were reading."

Her voice softened, but she didn't give in. "Regardless of why you did it, I'm asking you to back off. Please."

"You're holding all the cards, Clare, so what you want goes. But this whole time we've been standing here talking about Tim and what he needs and how he's going to get hurt not once did you mention Allie or how she's going to feel at the end of this. You dragged her into mediation, into your life, basically. Are you going to lay down the law when she and Tim are close enough?"

She put a hand up and held the neck of her jacket closed. Her cheeks were red from the wind.

"I will certainly try to consider Allie's feelings," she said, her voice tight. "Same as I'm asking you to consider Tim's."

"Thanks." He walked away. He half expected her to come after him, but she didn't. He was fuming and he wasn't even sure why. He couldn't believe she didn't want him to get closer to her son. Whatever it was he couldn't understand must be damn intense because she wasn't backing down, but, man, he was pissed.

It was Erin all over again. He wasn't allowed to be part of Tim's life—Clare knew best and his feelings didn't matter. The pathetic thing was, a whole bunch of parents would happily pay him to give their kids hockey tips, but Clare didn't believe his interaction was worth it for her son.

When he reached the car, he knocked on the back window before he got in his seat. Inside it was warm and the radio was blasting a song he recognized from the top-forty station Allie programmed into the number-one preset every time she got into the car even though he reprogrammed it with his classic rock every time he drove alone. He pressed the volume control on the steering wheel until he could hear himself.

"Your mom's waiting for you."

"Can we drive Tim home?" Allie asked.

Bryan clenched his teeth. This. This was exactly why Clare's boundaries were unfair to everyone in this stupid pact. His kid never asked to spend time with other kids. Allie was being set up for pain just as sure as Tim was. They all were.

"Not today, Allie," he said. "You better run, Tim. Your mom said something about taking you for new sneakers."

"Yes! See you, Allie," Tim said. "Bye, Bryan."

There. Let Clare deal with that. He hoped she got stuck buying the sneakers. He was going to take his daughter home and forget about everything else. In fact…

"You want to go to Gusti's, grab some pizza?" he asked Allie.

"It's not Friday."

He looked at her. "So?" he said. "We deserve a pizza for our excellent mediation progress."

She hesitated, obviously not sure what was going on.

"Come on, Allie. Let's take a break from all this crap. I'll buy you a root beer and we'll see if they'll make us a brownie à la mode. Let's live a little."

"Okay," she said. She pulled her seat belt on and sank back into her seat. "Sounds good."

LATER THAT WEEK, BRYAN WAS checking into a motel outside Erie when his phone rang. He handed his credit card to the teenage clerk and glanced at the caller ID.

"Excuse me," he said to the kid behind the counter. "I have to take this."

While the clerk ran his card through the machine and opened a drawer to pull out a card key, Bryan opened his phone. "Mary? What's up?"

"This isn't working anymore, Bryan." His sister sounded even more stressed than usual. Mary had four kids and her husband worked long hours as a contractor. He used to make fun of her constant chaos over the kids' schedules, but then Erin left and he'd found out how hard being a full-time parent was. He'd stopped teasing his sister and started bringing takeout whenever he got back to town at dinnertime. "It's too much for me to handle."

"Slow down, what's going on?"

"She attacked Lisa. Bryan, my daughter has a fat lip. I can't take her issues on top of everything else I have to deal with."

He pressed a hand to his forehead. He couldn't believe what Mary was saying. How could Allie have...

"You have to come get her."

"Mary, I'm four hours away."

"I'll wait up."

"I have meetings the rest of the week."

He heard a door slam on her end and he guessed she'd gone out to the garage. Allie had told him once that Aunt Mary kept a secret stash of Ho Hos out there. It was also one of the only places she could count on privacy.

"Listen, Bryan. I told you I'd help in any way I can, but this is too much. We agreed to one week of travel a month and this is the second month when you've been gone more than that."

"You're right," he said. "I'm sorry. I'll do better. I'll get—"

"No," his sister said. She no longer sounded angry. That was how her moods worked—her anger blew out as quickly as it flared up. This Mary, the one who wasn't mad, but just telling it like it is, was more intimidating. She was eight years older than him and he'd never lost the habit of doing exactly what she said. "Look, I didn't want to tell you this because I know how hard you're trying to keep things together for Allie."

So don't tell me, Bryan thought. Don't.

"But the girls don't get along anymore. Allie is so different from Lisa and they're at each other's throats all the time. It's cruel to keep throwing them together like this."

"I'm not *throwing them together*. I'm asking you to

watch your niece for a couple days when I travel. She doesn't have to hang out with Lisa."

"But it's more than a couple days. When she's here—you know how small the house is—they can't avoid each other. They're in the same classes at school. She has to share Lisa's room. She sees Lisa living this different life, with…things in it that Allie doesn't have. If I make Lisa take her along with her friends, they're both miserable but if Allie stays home, I feel like a jerk. Girls this age can be brutal, Bryan. I…you have to figure out a different situation or…"

"Or what, Mary?"

"I don't know," she said, sounding frustrated. "Stop traveling? How many times does it have to be the thing that screws everything up before you realize you have to quit it?"

"Quit my job?"

"Quit using your job as an excuse to spend half your time gone like Dad did. You can find another job, Bryan. Erin made it hard for you to be home, but she's not here now. You are. You have to take care of this."

"How is quitting my job going to take care of anything?"

"How is the way your daughter is living now good for her? Erin's not coming back to Twin Falls, don't kid yourself about that. If you don't want her to take Allie, you have to get a more permanent arrangement."

Bryan was breathing as hard as if he'd just skated sprints. What the hell was he supposed to change? Mary was… He wanted to blame her, Lord, how he wanted to blame her. But even though his sister was stressed and sometimes short-tempered she loved him. And she loved Allie. Hell, she even loved Erin. If Mary said she couldn't watch Allie this much, he had to accept it.

Accept it and do what? He had no freaking clue.

"Okay. But, Mary, I can't come home tonight. You're going to have to keep her."

"I can't. She's miserable, Bryan. Lisa is the one sporting the black eye, but Allie's the one who's hurting. She wants you to come home."

She wants you to come home.

When had anyone ever said that about him? He couldn't count the number of times he'd called Erin and told her he was going to extend a trip and she'd never once asked him to come back early.

He could go home. If he pushed it, he could be there by midnight. But then what? When Mary said Allie needed him, she didn't mean just him physically in the room.

Between Erie and home he was going to have to figure out some next steps because his last backup had taken herself out of the game.

"Tell her—" he paused. "Tell her to pack her stuff. Tell her I'm coming."

Mary hung up and Bryan went back to the desk. He wondered how Allie would feel when she got that message. What part of "your dad's on his way" could possibly comfort her? She'd asked for him to come, though.

The clerk looked irritated that he had to unprocess the credit card, but Bryan barely noticed. He was preoccupied with Allie. When he was a kid, on nights his dad was due home from a trip for his own sales job, he'd sometimes played a game with himself. He'd pretend to go to bed but then when his sister and his mom were asleep, he'd get up again. He'd stuff a blanket against the bottom of his door to block the crack and then he'd turn on his lights and sit in the hard chair at his desk and wait.

He didn't let himself read or listen to music or move from the chair. He never fell asleep. Not one single time. His dad would pull into the driveway and then Bryan would hear the slam of the car door. When he put his suitcase down in the front hall, the zipper would make a metallic clink on the tile floor. His dad almost always stopped in the kitchen where he'd fix himself an Alka-Seltzer before heading upstairs.

The second his dad's foot hit the bottom riser, Bryan would flick the lights off and jump back into bed. His dad never opened his door and Bryan never let him find out he was awake. He'd never really known why he was staying up. It wasn't because he wanted to talk to his dad—they didn't do that. Not the kind of talking people would do in the middle of the night, anyway. In the morning his dad would quiz him about his practice schedule and he'd look over the workout sheets Bryan filled out each day. They'd discuss stats and strategy, but there'd never been a reason to stay up late for any of that. It was always waiting in the morning.

He grabbed the handle of his suitcase and draped his laptop bag across his shoulder as he headed back out to where he'd left the Lexus in the space next to the door.

Was it a vigil? Had he feared there might be a time when his dad wouldn't come home from a trip? He wondered if there hadn't been some little kid part of him that sensed things weren't good between his parents, that worried there wasn't much tying his dad to them. Maybe when he waited up for his dad, he'd been trying to show the guy it mattered if he came back. Except in his family you didn't tell someone they mattered.

Bryan couldn't say why he'd stayed up all those nights waiting for his dad. After he grew up and started traveling for his own work, he'd gone into Allie's room every single time he came home late. Erin would tell him he shouldn't bother Allie, but in this he hadn't let her stop him. He'd straighten his daughter's covers and pull the pillow back square under her head. She liked to wrap herself in her blankets like a cocoon, and he'd tuck her in tighter, imagining she felt the blankets around her like a hug. Before he left he'd lean his forehead against hers and whisper that he loved her. Sometimes she woke up enough to whisper back.

HE PULLED INTO Mary's driveway a little before midnight. He was dead tired but wired from worry. After he'd been in the warm car that long, the cold was so fierce he felt it deep in his lungs. He glanced up at the sky, where the stars were glittering bright and unreachable. He saw no signs in them. If his dad's soul was up there somewhere, the guy was as uncommunicative as he'd always been.

Clare would figure this out, he thought. If he asked her for help. She'd give him and Allie that look, her smart eyes flashing behind her glasses, and her mouth held in a straight line, but her irritation wouldn't last and in a minute she'd be smiling again and telling them how to be the kind of family where everything worked. She could tidy them up the same way she'd taken care of the conversation about the mural in the party room.

Yeah, right. Clare would have to admit he and Allie mattered enough to figure out his problems first.

He'd called his sister a few minutes ago. As he walked up on the porch he heard her coming down the stairs, so he didn't ring the bell. When Mary let him in she leaned over to scoop a basket full of her kids' gloves and hats back into the closet, giving him a view into the living room. A table lamp glowed in the far corner, but otherwise the downstairs was dark. Allie was slumped on the couch, her duffel bag next to her, one arm bent, propping up her head. Her eyes were closed, her long hair pushed forward to cover the left side of her face. She looked about seven years old.

"I told her she should get in bed, but she wanted to wait for you. She didn't say it, but she was really happy you were coming."

He swallowed.

Mary pushed her hands through her hair, leaving it standing up on top. He'd called her rooster when she was taking high-school French because her hair was always sticking up. She was wearing an oversize Sabres T-shirt and a pair of pajama bottoms that probably belonged to her husband. Without her makeup she looked older. Tired. "I wish I hadn't had to call, Bryan."

"I know."

"She's a good kid."

He looked at her and said sharply, "I *know.*"

"Okay."

He ran a hand over his jaw. "Sorry. I'm on edge."

"It's okay, Bryan."

He took a step toward the living room.

"Did you call Erin?" Mary asked, keeping her voice low.

"No," he said. He hadn't even tried her. He'd temporarily panicked, but he hadn't called Erin. He'd even scraped together a semirespectable game plan for Allie the next couple of days. Granted it wasn't a very good plan and he wouldn't be able to use it after this one time, but he'd straightened it all out on the drive back and it would work for a few days.

He hadn't called Erin.

It'd be nice if he could be sure he hadn't called because he was getting better at being in charge, but he wondered if he hadn't unconsciously given up on getting her to help.

"What are you going to do?"

He smiled. An inappropriate reaction, because this wasn't a joking situation, but he couldn't help it. He'd had a crisis and he hadn't called Erin. He considered that a win.

"Road trip!"

Mary put her hands on her hips, suddenly more awake. "You can't take her with you—she has school."

"I canceled a couple appointments. I only have to cover two days."

"Two days when she's supposed to be in school."

"Two days off isn't going to kill her."

"She'll be bored."

"She'll deal with it."

"What about hockey?"

"Mary, please." He grabbed her hands and held on carefully. She was the one who had made him come home, wasn't she? "I'm doing the best I can. For this week, for this time, I'm taking her with me."

His sister bit back whatever she'd been about to say. "Good. Okay. You'll be fine."

He sighed, looking at his daughter camped on the

couch. "I don't suppose we can get much worse. Too bad Mom doesn't live here anymore."

"She never liked Erin. Can you imagine what she'd say about all this?" Their mom had moved to a condo in South Carolina a few years ago. Bryan had thought about asking her to come back to help with Allie, but she hated the cold and would be miserable. He needed a long-term solution.

He crossed the living room and touched Allie's shoulder. "Allie? Honey?"

It took a few seconds for her to rouse herself. When she eventually looked up, her eyes were unfocused, but she smiled at him. Her smile had been so rare recently that he drank it in, smiling back. Remembering all those other nights when he'd come home and she'd woken up to see him.

"Let's go," he said, guiding her into her jacket, tugging her knit Twin Falls Cowboys hat on her head and then picking her bag up before steering her forward.

He leaned past her to open the door but she pulled back, twisting a chunk of her hair around her finger nervously. "I'm sorry, Aunt Mary."

"Oh, Allie, of course you are, sweetie."

"I tried to tell Lisa sorry, but she didn't open the door. I wrote her a note." She pulled a much-folded piece of paper from her pocket.

"I'll give it to her." Mary put her hands on Allie's shoulders. "I'm sorry, too, Allie."

Bryan gave his sister a quick, one-armed hug and then helped Allie out the door. He gripped her elbow through the sleeve of her ski jacket. She was awake enough to manage the walk on her own, but once he'd grabbed her, he didn't want to let go. She didn't pull away, either.

He got her into the car and buckled himself in, ready to drive back to the apartment. He'd planned to stay there tonight and then head out early in the morning, but he wasn't tired anymore, and he really didn't want to go to the apartment. If they went there they'd fall right into their normal patterns. How could they ever make a new start?

He turned to Allie, but she was leaning on the door, her eyes closed again.

They kept a fleece blanket, a sample from a supplier, in the backseat. He tucked it in around Allie and then turned the radio on to his favorite classic-rock station. With Bruce Springsteen's low rumbling "Born to Run" thrumming in the speakers, Bryan headed for the Interstate.

CHAPTER NINE

"DAD!"

Allie's voice pulled him out of sleep. He was disoriented, sluggish, unsure where he was for the moment. He sat up and the details of the motel room became clear. The clock on the nightstand read eight-fifteen. Allie was on the other bed, covered by the blankets, only her eyes and a sliver of her nose showing. She looked impossibly small.

"Where are we?"

"Erie. Days Inn."

"Why?"

"Aunt Mary called me and I came home to get you. I couldn't skip work, so I brought you with me."

"It's a school day."

"You're having a vacation." His voice, full of forced cheer, sounded so fake to him, but Allie hadn't taken her eyes off his face. He wondered what else she wanted to ask. "You doing okay?" he prompted.

She didn't respond, except to pull the covers tighter.

"My first appointment is in less than an hour. Can you get ready?"

She nodded and he pulled his toiletries kit out of his duffel and headed for the bathroom.

Leaning on the sink, he stared at his own tired face. *Awesome, Bryan. Way to connect with the kid.*

He straightened up. It was early. He had time.

Time didn't help. If anything, it made things worse. He and Allie were so uncomfortable with each other, neither of them knowing what to say, and the disconnect seemed to get worse the longer they spent together. After a day of appointments at two skate shops in Erie and one at a rink an hour south, and a dinner at Pizza Hut, during which he exchanged more conversation with the waitress than he did with Allie, they headed back to the hotel.

She sat on the end of her bed and he went into the bathroom to wash his face. He heard her sneakers drop one by one on the floor and then the television came on. One of the songs Allie had been playing nonstop for the past few weeks started as he splashed water on his face and rooted around looking for his toothbrush.

He dried his hands and then opened the bathroom door. Allie's hand jerked on the remote and she changed the channel so fast it seemed she was trying to hide something, but he was sure she'd been watching one of the entertainment-news channels. He'd seen the blonde with the big breasts who always reminded him of his seventh-grade English teacher. News about some pop band with a top-forty song might be inane, but it wasn't something to hide.

Unless...

"Was that Lush?" he asked. He couldn't believe he hadn't made the connection earlier. The band she'd been obsessing over was the one Erin was on tour with. Every single time they'd fought over the past two months, she'd retreated to her bedroom or the bathroom and turned on that same music. How could he have missed it?

"Sorry," she said.

"Sorry for what? It's okay if you want to watch them."

That was when she started to cry. She kept her head down and her hair was hiding her face so he didn't notice at first. But then her shoulder jerked and she dropped the remote onto the bed so she could cup her hands around her face. She wasn't sobbing, but somehow these quiet, desperate tears were worse. She didn't sound as if she could breathe.

"Allie—"

"I'm sorry," she choked. "I'm sorry."

He couldn't move. He should go to her, but he was in shock. She never cried. He couldn't remember the last time he'd seen her in tears.

"What's wrong?"

"I miss her. I really, really miss her."

She looked up, tears streaking her cheeks, her eyes dark and every inch of her miserable. Bryan sat next to her, pulling her into his side, not letting her pull away. He wrapped his other arm around her when she finally gave in and let him hold her.

He held her while she cried. He stroked her back and pushed her hair away from her wet, sweaty face, gently straightening the tangled strands and smoothing them on her shoulders. He patted her and every time she said she was sorry, he said not to worry.

She cried for a long time, her shoulders hitching and jerking under his hands. When her tears finally slowed down, he said, "I'm sorry, Allie. I know it sucks. But I also know Mom misses you."

"She doesn't."

"She does." Bryan pulled her closer and shifted her up so he could see her face. "She's busy and she's excited that she's getting to go after her dreams. But she does miss you."

"She always sounds happy when I talk to her." Allie's voice shook and new tears spilled. "I'm not happy at all, but she is. She always is."

He couldn't argue. Erin was happy. She was excited about her career and she was enjoying being on her own. She did miss Allie, but she was undeniably happy.

"It's different for her. She has so much new stuff going on, new people and her job, the band, everything is exciting," he said. "But you and me, we're trying to figure out how to keep on the way we always have but without Mom."

"But I'm *not* the same. That's the problem."

"What problem?"

"The problem with me. Why everyone hates me."

"What are you talking about?"

She shrugged out from under his arm. She moved a few feet away to sit in the chair next to the window with her legs drawn up in front of her, hands clasped around her knees.

"Nothing. Forget it. I'm fine."

He'd never been so happy that his company had a strict policy against the sales force staying in suites. If there'd been someplace to go Allie would have run, would have put a door between them again. She couldn't this time, though, and he was determined to push her until she let him in.

"I can't forget it, Allie. Who hates you?"

"I didn't mean to say that," she said, a little desperately. "I'm fine. I got in trouble again with Aunt Mary, but I'm sorry. It won't happen again."

"Hey, I'm worried about you, not mad."

She shook her head. "I don't want you to worry about me. I'm fine." She'd picked up a twist of her hair and was pulling the strands apart, separating them in her fist and then squeezing them back together.

This was getting them nowhere. If anything, she was digging in deeper. He slid across to the edge of the bed closest to her. Lowering himself to crouch in front of her, he ignored the tightness in his knee and made eye contact with her.

"You keep saying you're fine, but you're not. Which is okay—you don't have to be fine all the time. What's wrong?"

She shook her head again, but he wasn't sure she was aware she was doing it. Her eyes were locked on his. She needed something, but he couldn't tell what she was asking for.

"If…" she started, but tears caught in her throat and she had to pause to suck in a few deep breaths. "If I did everything right, I hoped it would be okay. That you wouldn't mind that you got stuck with me. But I can't. Nothing is like it was last year with me or school or Lisa or hockey or anything and I don't know what I'm supposed to do." Her voice rose but she reined it in again. "I keep messing up but it's not on purpose. It's not."

She put her hands over her mouth, pressing in with her fingers, and then said, "Every week at mediation, we talk about why I hit Tim and if I say I was angry, Lila wants to know why, but I don't even know. I just was! I just am."

He shifted so he was kneeling in front of her and leaned forward, putting his arms around her and tucking her head onto his shoulder. She cried again for so long that he realized she'd been wound much too tight for much too long.

He was an idiot. Why hadn't he forced this conversation two weeks ago or two months ago? Erin wasn't coming back to rescue him or raise their daughter. Not right now, anyway. His sister might be okay as an occasional backup, but she had her own kids and her own problems. He and Allie were in this together. Alone, but together. It was time for him to show up.

"I don't feel stuck with you, kiddo. Never that."

"I wish there was no such thing as puberty. Lisa—"

She stopped, but he couldn't let her off the hook.

"Lisa what?"

"Her friends say I'm a baby because I don't wear makeup and I don't have a boyfriend. They said I want to be a boy because I like hockey and that it's not normal to play with boys. They said I'm a freak and everyone knows it."

Bryan sat back on his heels. "Is that why you got in a fight?"

Allie folded her hands in her lap, rubbing her thumbs together nervously. "Is it normal I don't want a boyfriend?"

"Normal? It's completely normal," Bryan said. God, what would he do when she wanted a boyfriend? This was much better. Perfect, even. Except Allie wasn't happy. He might be overjoyed if his daughter never dated anyone until well after college graduation, but it had to be what she wanted, and right now she didn't look convinced. "Allie, everybody grows up different. Lisa might be interested in boys, but that doesn't make her better than you—just different. It's okay for you to take your time if that's what you want."

She nodded. Was she actually listening to him? He hoped he was saying the right things.

"I never had a girlfriend until I met your mom."

"You didn't?"

"Nope. I was too into hockey to notice girls." He might not even have noticed Erin if he hadn't moved into her house when he boarded out for junior hockey.

"I bet Mom had lots of boyfriends."

"She had a couple, but your aunt Mary didn't even have a date for her senior prom. She went with our cousin David. She lied and told everyone he was her boyfriend from summer camp. She had to pay him twenty dollars."

Allie stopped fiddling with her hair and studied his face. "Seriously?"

"I value my life, kiddo. I would never make up an unflattering story about your aunt Mary," he said. "It's totally normal to take your time with big changes. Give yourself a break, right? And give me a heads-up when things are going wrong."

"I don't want to be a pain."

He laughed. It wasn't funny, but she had no clue how much better he felt now that he had some details about what was going on with her. "Letting me know what's bothering you is not being a pain. I can't help if I don't know what's up."

She nodded, but she still didn't relax.

"Look." He stood, stretching his back while he gave himself a beat to plan his words. "I love you. You mean more to me than anyone in the world. That's clear, right?"

She nodded again, maybe this time with more understanding, maybe even a little hope.

"But you're complicated, kid. You have so much going on that I can't even guess at. You have to keep talking to me so I can help."

She blushed. "I'm not complicated."

"All women are complicated." She opened her mouth to protest so he held up a hand. "I know you're not a woman yet and I'm just as happy for you to stay a girl for a few more years. But you're in training, like it or not, and that means you're complicated." She smiled, her hold on her knees loosening. "You have to cut me some slack and talk to me."

"I will. Promise."

"And no more hitting people," he said. "I mean it, Allie. Lila is goofy, but she seems to know what she's doing. She'll teach you how to deal with your emotions when you're angry, but you have to learn it."

"I will."

He checked her over. She looked like crap. Her face was red and blotched with tears, her hair was hanging in damp tangles and the front of her t-shirt was a mess. But the scared look she'd had in her eyes for weeks was gone and a little of her old sparkle was back. She was almost smiling, the corners of her mouth lifting and the worry lines that had taken up residence in her forehead gone. Beautiful.

"Shake?" He held out his hand. She grabbed it, but then used it to pull herself out of the chair and wrap her arms around his waist.

"I love you, Dad." She pressed her head against his chest. "Thanks for coming to pick me up."

"Always, Allie. Any time, any where."

She headed into the bathroom and he heard the water turn on for the shower. He sat in the chair she'd left, leaning his head against the wall. Man, he was wiped out. Maybe between him and Lila they could help her figure things out, get back on track.

Damn. Lila.

Allie had a mediation session tomorrow and he had appointments until midafternoon. No way they'd be back in time to make it. It was late, but he called her office number and left a message. She'd hear it in the morning and he'd call at some point and reschedule. He was about to close his eyes for a quick nap when he realized that Clare wouldn't know he'd canceled the appointment. She had a full schedule and probably had to make arrangements to get Tim to the center. If Lila didn't touch base with her before Tim went to school it could mess up her whole day.

Clare already believed he and Allie were a pair of screwups—he didn't want any more grief from her.

He banged on the door to the bathroom and told Allie he had to step out for a few minutes. In the hallway he hesitated. He didn't want to go down to the lobby, because there was no chance of privacy there, but he couldn't stay here outside the room. Sound carried and he didn't want Allie to hear him. As long as he was calling Clare, he had a question he wanted to ask her.

He walked to the end of the hall and pushed open the door to the staircase. The stairs were wide and carpeted with that green stuff that always reminded him of AstroTurf. He sat and scrolled through his contacts until he found Clare's number. While the phone was dialing, his stomach started jumping the same way it had when he was a teenager calling some girl for a date.

How ironic was it that he'd just finished dealing with

his daughter's teenage anxiety and now he was acting like a kid about calling Clare?

THE PHONE RANG as Clare was putting Tim's lunch bag in the fridge. She hated packing lunches, because she had yet to find a satisfactory menu that was both easy to transport and still appetizing. She wished Tim would eat in the cafeteria at school more often, but he told her it was a waste of time to try to figure out the lunch lines and menu choices since he was only going to be there for one year. He was punishing her, but since he was the one who had to put up with soggy sandwiches and crushed cookies, she kept hoping he'd get tired of his protest.

When Bryan's name came up on the caller ID, her spirits rose. Not because she wanted to talk to him, she told herself, but because now she had an excuse for not moving on to sorting through the papers in Tim's backpack, which was her next task. The last time she'd looked through it, in addition to all the PTA notices and crumpled homework sheets, she found two pieces of correspondence that Lindsey later termed "mash notes." Tim denied all knowledge of anyone named Juliana. Clare wasn't looking forward to what she might find this time.

"Bryan?"

He didn't answer right away. Thank goodness for modern technology like caller ID.

"Clare, hi." There was another short pause. "I wanted to call you because Allie won't be able to make it to the mediation meeting tomorrow. I left a message for Lila but I didn't know when she'd get in touch with you and I thought it might be better if you knew tonight."

"Oh. Okay." When he didn't immediately try to break off the connection, she scrambled for something to say. "She's not sick, is she?"

He cleared his throat. She could see him in her mind, doing that thing he did where he looked down at his hands while he gathered his thoughts. She liked that he didn't leap in too quickly before he spoke.

"No," he said. "Could I ask you something?"

"Sure."

"Okay. Uh, this is awkward," he said. "Does Tim have a girlfriend?"

He was right. This was awkward.

"Your guess is as good as mine," she said. "Mary's daughter is writing poems about him, but he doesn't talk about her. Someone named Juliana sends him notes, but he told me to recycle them. Why?"

"I wondered if there was any chance that what happened between Allie and Tim was because of something like that."

Clare almost choked. "Something like what?"

"Like boy-girl stuff."

"Like she likes him?"

"Or he likes her," he said. "It's possible. I'm just speculating."

Missing pieces fell into place. Tim's adamant refusal to tell her what was going on. His insistence that Allie wasn't bullying him, that the fights were a misunderstanding. The cologne. The way Tim was willing to go along with whatever Allie said.

"Interesting theory."

"Interesting kids," he answered. "Listen, I realize we're not exactly friends. But you're the only one who knows everything about what's been going on with Allie.

Anyone else, if I talked to them, they might get a worse opinion of her, but you…" His voice trailed off.

"Bryan, I don't have a bad opinion of Allie. I know the details of some situations she's been involved in and I certainly have issues with her behavior, but my opinion is that Allie is a kid who's having a rough time and is maybe a bit lost."

Huh. She wasn't sure when she'd started to change her mind about Allie.

"Thanks, Clare. I didn't expect that."

"Honestly, I didn't either." She smiled.

"Allie got in another fight, this time with her cousin Lisa, Mary's daughter. I had to go and pick her up because my sister couldn't keep her, so we're here on my road trip together. That's why she won't be at mediation."

Clare sat on the floor of the kitchen. She put the solid plaster wall at her back. Her first feeling was horror. How out of control was Allie? But she remembered Bryan checking her over that first night after she'd fought with Tim. Allie was Bryan's baby and she wanted to respect that.

"How are you doing?"

He sighed. "I wish I knew. She talked to me finally. That was good, but I'm out of my depth here."

"Want to tell me what she said?"

"What I want is to wind back the timeline about seven years to when Allie was in first grade and her biggest worry was whether the tooth fairy was going to show up."

He sounded exhausted.

"Teenagers are hard, Bryan."

"I was hoping that was true," he answered. "I was hoping it wasn't me and Allie."

"Not all of them are as challenging as her, but they all have their moments."

"But you and Tim are close, right? You guys seem to have figured things out."

She wanted to say yes, wanted it in the worst way. But it wasn't true, and hadn't been true since she'd told him they were moving again.

"We're okay mostly, but this year has been difficult."

"Thank God."

"What?"

"Sorry. Not thank God you're having problems. Thank God I'm not the only one."

He was so disarmingly honest sometimes.

"But you said she talked to you?"

"She's having a hard time because everything is changing and she isn't ready for it, I guess. Her cousin is into boys and it sounds like the girls in their class are teasing Allie pretty hard because she doesn't want a boyfriend. I guess with Allie, hurt and confused come out mad."

"Thirteen isn't easy for anybody," she said.

"That's good to know," Bryan said. He didn't sound as nervous as he'd been when she first answered. "I definitely didn't get into girls until I was older. Maybe I played so much hockey I missed this stuff when it first started."

"It starts earlier now, but it's always the girls who get to it first."

"You sound like you speak from experience. Were you kissing boys when you were thirteen?"

The year she'd turned thirteen, Gretchen had been in the hospital for a month with pneumonia and then in bed at home for several more months with recurrences and complications. Her parents had been out of their minds with worry.

For her birthday, Lindsey had given her a gift certificate to get her ears pierced at the mall, but her parents had a fit about the possibility she'd get an infection and she hadn't been allowed. She still remembered how hard she'd had to bite back her envy when Lindsey had showed off her first pair of gold studs.

Her sister had asked her parents to get Clare a copy of *Are You There God? It's Me, Margaret* for her birthday. The two of them read the book over the course of one long Saturday. They'd alternately giggled, ew'ed and wondered over Judy Blume's classic story of a girl taking her first steps toward adulthood. Neither of them had ever had a birds-and-bees conversation from their mother, and Clare had been pitifully uninformed about her own body when she went away to college.

She'd read about coming-of-age ceremonies women did with their daughters to celebrate that transition from childhood. She wondered if an approach like that might help Allie find her footing. Her mouth went dry. A coming-of-age ceremony would be shared with people who were important to you—a mother, a favorite aunt— not some lady you met because you'd punched out her son. Which was all she was to Allie.

"I wasn't much like Allie when I was thirteen," she said abruptly. She rarely told people about Gretchen, preferring to keep her memories to herself. Other people always asked questions that made Clare feel as if she was talking behind her sister's back.

"Listen, I should go. Allie's alone in the room," he said. Her tone didn't seem to have registered with him. "But thanks. Thanks for letting me talk to you."

She wanted to tell him she was there for him anytime he wanted to talk, but that wasn't true. She was here for only a few months and then she was moving on. She'd never know if Allie worked out her issues or if Bryan started to trust his instincts with his daughter. When Tim was finally old enough to start dating, Allie and Lisa and the mysterious Juliana were going to be distant memories, if that. She had to put this relationship back into the right context. "I want the mediation to work as much as you."

"The mediation," he said, his voice flat.

"Well, that's why we're spending time together, right? Allie gets to skate and Tim doesn't get any more black eyes."

The words hung there, awkward and forced.

"Right. Thanks again." He hung up.

She put the phone down on the counter and leaned over the sink to look out the window. The spotlight in the backyard lit up fat drifting flakes. More snow. She shivered.

She'd hurt him again. He'd reached out and she'd brought their relationship back to the mediation agreement. It had been the right move. She couldn't get in the habit of counting on Bryan and she certainly didn't want him to get in the habit of counting on her.

It had been nice to talk to him, though. She'd often wondered what it would be like to share her concerns over Tim with his dad. Matteo had never been very involved in their lives. He took Tim every summer—there was never any hesitation about the trip and Tim always seemed to have fun. But he didn't engage her about their lives during the year. She talked to Lindsey, but Bryan was different.

He was kind and thoughtful and trusted her opinion. She wished she could call him back and tell him more about her worries over Tim. Maybe he could explain what it was like to be a seventh-grade boy. What if he was right and Tim liked Allie? What if they went on a date? Were there dances in seventh grade? Probably not the kind you needed a date for, but in a few years there'd be a prom. If Allie and Tim went together, she could imagine Bryan driving them and then maybe coming back to her place while the kids were out.

Clare smacked her hand on the counter. She was in over her head here. She wasn't staying in Twin Falls. She wasn't going to let Bryan and Allie into her heart any deeper than they already were.

But where would she be when Tim went to the prom? Would his date be a stranger to her? A near stranger to him?

She went upstairs to her desk and pulled out the rental agreement for the tenants in her house in Seattle. They were signed through the end of June.

She sat in the chair at her desk. She opened the locked bottom drawer of the desk and lifted out the file containing her will and their passports and birth certificates. Underneath was a scrapbook. She had two pictures from her childhood that she kept out—one was of her and Gretchen on the deck of the boat shuttle that ran between Seattle and Vancouver. Gretchen was about eleven and no one looking at the picture would know she'd already started feeling the physical effects of her disease. They were arm in arm, smiling and waving at the camera with the sun glinting on the ocean behind them. She'd framed that picture for Tim when he was born.

The other picture was older. It was the day her parents brought her home from the hospital. Gretchen was propped up in a big, flowered chair, holding her. Her mom and dad were crouched next to the chair, supporting her. Clare liked that picture because of Gretchen's expression. She looked so proud of herself. Even when she'd been increasingly dependent on Clare or her parents for her daily needs, she'd never relinquished her role as big sister. It had been Gretchen who demanded that Clare be allowed to go to college out of state. Their collaborations on application essays and forms and then the shared excitement as Clare's acceptance letters had come in sustained Gretchen during what turned out to be her last few months. She died two weeks after Clare moved into her dorm at Stanford.

Clare opened the scrapbook. She kept her private memories here. The first page was a picture of the exterior of the Seattle house. The tulips in the yard were in full bloom and Clare's breath caught at the sight of so much sunshine.

She turned the page and looked at the pictures from her early childhood. She'd done this so many times before—examining each photo, searching for the signs someone should have seen that would have told them sooner that Gretchen was ill, but she never saw anything. For ten years, Gretchen had grown up as normal as any other child. As ordinary as her sister.

Clare closed the book before she got too far, but then she opened it again and took the house picture off the first page. She closed the scrapbook and put everything back in the drawer, locking it. She propped the picture of the house on the windowsill. The contrast between the sunny spring in the picture and the blowing cold outside was stark.

If she and Tim did settle somewhere, it was logical to go to Seattle. Lindsey was there. The house she owned was there. Maybe she could handle it, live in Seattle long enough for Tim to get through high school. She'd find the courage to let him make connections with people, to put down those roots he wanted that scared her to death. Once he was in college, she could always pick up stakes again.

A deer walked slowly through the circle of light cast by the spotlight in the backyard. She imagined herself twenty years from now, in this same position. Coming to the end of a contract, putting out feelers and looking for a new gig in another new town.

She'd have no idea if Bryan and Allie figured out their issues or if Allie had come through this trouble and emerged on the other side happy and successful. If that did happen, it would have nothing to do with her anyway.

Seattle was the logical choice. If she could bring herself to make this step. She moved the picture of the house, settling it against a row of books on her desk. Outside the window, snow continued to drift in lazy circles. For the first time in a long time, she took no comfort from knowing she'd found the logical solution to a problem.

CHAPTER TEN

THEIR FIRST CLEANING session for the party room at the rink was scheduled for Sunday night. The kids had asked to work during hours when they would be less likely to run into any of their teammates.

Clare had spent the afternoon on a conference call with her group from work. The project was ahead of schedule and she had a feeling she might be working herself out of a contract before the scheduled deadline. She'd get paid the whole fee, so they could manage the finances to stay here to let Tim finish out the year—she just couldn't imagine how she'd spend her time without work to take her mind off everything else.

When the call ended, she was on edge so she called Lindsey to see if her friend wanted to fly out for a few days. The hockey team had a tournament at the end of February and Clare hoped Tim might like it if his godmother could see him play. They agreed to talk again about the details, but Lindsey said they should count on her.

"I have to go, Lindsey," she said. "We're cleaning the party room tonight."

"Oh. Sorry about that. I hope it goes well."

"I wish the kids picked something different, like, I don't know, a skate-a-thon."

Lindsey snorted. "You don't skate."

That was true, but ever since she'd watched those YouTube videos of Bryan, she'd been wondering what it would feel like.

She didn't want to get into a discussion about skating with Lindsey so she said, "With a skate-a-thon, there wouldn't be a reason for Bryan to wear his tool belt."

"He has a tool belt?"

Clare nodded. She leaned back in her chair. "I haven't seen it yet, but he's that kind of guy. He's going to be competent and strong and he already looks fantastic in his jeans but with the tool belt, it's going to be like working with some kind of sexy calendar model. I'm doomed."

Lindsey was staring at her through the monitor. "That's a lot of pent-up resentment toward a tool belt that may or may not even exist."

"It exists. Trust me."

"I thought you were definitely not getting involved with him."

"Oh, I'm not. Definitely not. My mind is perfectly clear on that. It's my body that's not completely on board with the decision. The tool belt is going to fan the flames."

Lindsey raised an eyebrow. "If he puts it on, send me a picture."

"Find your own calendar stud," Clare said. They signed off and she shut her computer down. She stuck her head around the corner and yelled down to Tim to get up and moving, but he didn't answer.

"Tim!" she yelled again. "Don't make me walk down there every time I want to talk to you."

Still no answer.

She started stomping down the hall, hoping he'd

hear her coming and ask what she wanted, but when she passed his bathroom, she heard the shower running. The unmistakable aroma of that horrible body wash drifted out on the steam from under the door.

She stared. He was showering just to go to the rink to clean out a storage area?

How had Bryan put it? A boy-girl thing?

She went back to her room and flipped the lever for her own shower. She was aware of the irony, but knowing the tool belt was coming, she had to attempt to look good. A level playing field might make it easier to resist him.

"YOU'VE GOT TO BE kidding," Clare said, snapping the words off in that way that Bryan had learned meant she was peeved. At least for once her anger wasn't directed at him. "Tim, you're sorely deluded if you imagine Mr. James and I are going to be stuck with all the heavy lifting while you and Allie go in the other room and color."

"We're working on the sketch for the collage, Mom, not coloring." Tim didn't seem particularly upset about how Clare was talking to him. "Besides, you agreed to do what we say. We came to a consensus on that."

Tim snuck a sideways look at Allie who gave him the barest hint of a nod.

"Well, Mr. James and I are in consensus that we're going to retool the division of labor."

Both Sampsons turned to Bryan. He'd kept an eye on Allie, who hadn't said a word, but had been following the exchange closely. Lila had told him that she'd hoped to boost Allie's confidence by putting the kids in charge.

"I'm ready to tackle the tasks I've been assigned." He paused and caught Tim's eye. "Sir."

Allie made a noise that sounded a lot as if she was stifling a laugh. Tim kept a straight face, but his eyes were dancing as he asked his mother, "Are you going to continue to try to subvert the agreement that we all, you included, signed?"

Clare threw her hands up. "If there's anything this group doesn't have room for, it's more subversives. Fine. Mr. James and I will work in here while you and Allie color."

Tim scooped up the file folder the kids had started with ideas for the photo wall.

"Allie," Bryan called. She turned and he tossed her the sketch pad he'd bought earlier that day at the art supply store. He'd been appalled at the price of the pad—it was only paper, wasn't it? Allie's delighted grin made the cost seem more than reasonable.

The kids closed the door and he was alone in the storage space with Clare.

"You sold me out," she said.

"Sure did." He'd do it again in a heartbeat if it meant he'd get to see Allie smile one more time.

The corners of her mouth curved up and he knew she wasn't really upset. "You might as well put your tool belt on."

"What?"

"You brought your tool belt, didn't you?"

"Yeah, but we're just cleaning."

Why was she looking at him like that? As if he was on the menu.

"Humor me."

He picked the tool belt up off the stack of boxes where

he'd dropped it when he walked in, but he hesitated. "Put it on now?"

She nodded.

He shrugged and buckled the leather belt around his waist, tugging it low until it sat comfortably on his hips. When it was fastened, he looked back at her. She was still watching him. She swallowed and then adjusted her glasses.

"That's exactly how I imagined it would look." She sighed and then muttered, "Next thing I know you're going to build something."

"Clare?" he asked.

"Don't mind me. Is there any music? I could use a distraction."

He went out to Danny's office and scrounged up a radio. When he came back through the lobby, Allie and Tim were on opposite sides of one of the café tables. She had a marker in her hand and looked to be sketching something. Tim, head propped on one hand, was watching her work.

When he got back to the storage room, Clare had taken off her sweater and was pushing up the sleeves on her bright pink V-neck T-shirt. He liked the way that T-shirt showed off her body. Her breasts were small but round and enticing. She lifted a stack of old magazines off a shelf and pivoted, looking for the garbage can.

He shoved the can over and steadied it while she dumped the magazines in. He took advantage of the opportunity to stand too close, letting his thigh rub against hers and feeling the curve of her bottom against him.

"How are the kids doing?" she asked.

"Tim's gazing at Allie. She's drawing."

"Maybe we should leave the door open," she said.

"It is a little stuffy in here."

"Right," she said, but he realized from the slight blush on her neck that she was embarrassed. She must have wanted the door open so they could keep an eye on the kids.

"He's just gazing, Clare," he said. "And they are supposed to be working together, remember?"

"It won't hurt to keep the door open."

"What are you afraid of? That she's going to attack him again?"

"No." Clare met his eyes. "It's not that. I want to keep track of what's going on."

"Why?" Bryan said sharply. "If anything does go on, it's not going to last long enough to get serious. So what's the problem?"

"Leave it closed, then," she said. "Since you know so much about kids."

He turned away from her, but he didn't open the door.

LINDSEY WOULD KILL HER for this one. Everything had been going well. The tool belt, in particular, was outstanding.

Then she had to step in it and insult him again. She had wanted the door open not just to keep an eye on the kids, but to remind herself that she had to be careful around Bryan. When he'd been standing so close to her before, she couldn't resist leaning into him the slightest bit and even that small contact of her jeans on his had woken up nerve endings her old boyfriend Vince had never even discovered.

They worked quietly for about twenty minutes, being extra polite and emphasizing the "excuse me's" when they passed each other carrying boxes and full garbage bags out to stack by the parking-lot door. She had her back to him when she heard him drop something heavy and then swear under his breath.

"Bryan?"

"What?" he snapped.

He leaned down to pick up a box full of old catalogs. He winced when he took a step toward the door and had to rest the box on the edge of a filing cabinet.

"Are you okay?"

"I twisted my knee. It'll be fine in a second."

"Want me to help you with that? We could take some of the magazines out and make two trips."

"It's fine," he repeated. Then he lifted the box and stomped out of the room. Well, *stomped* wasn't exactly the word, but she didn't know how to describe him stomping with his good leg and limping every other step on his other one. Maybe angry limping? Whatever, she was waiting for him when he came back.

She'd found a filing cabinet and got busy taking the old papers out of the drawers and loading them into cardboard boxes ready to go to the recycling center. She couldn't stand the strain between them. Her plan was to try the sideways talking she used with Tim. Maybe it was helpful with prickly adult men the way it was with prickly young ones.

Before she had a chance to try, he apologized.

"Sorry I snapped at you. I was mad at myself."

She forgot all about the sideways approach and spun around to face him.

He was such a confusing person. The jock label only fit him until he opened his mouth. Then he was not only an incredibly thoughtful person, he was considerate and loyal and genuinely nice. And she was surprised to find that those things were infinitely sexier than the tool belt that fit him just right. Although the tool belt was an awfully attractive bonus.

"Don't worry about it," she said.

They finished clearing the trash from the room and she started sweeping the cobwebs out of the corners while he climbed on a table to take down the blinds that covered the windows high on the outside wall. They weren't talking much, but the quiet didn't hold the edgy politeness from before. She kept an eye on him but his knee didn't seem to give him much trouble. She must not have been as circumspect as she'd hoped because as the deejay announced he was starting a block of Allman Brothers songs and the first strains of "Blue Sky" came on, Bryan said, "It wasn't hockey. People assume I wrecked my knee skating since it ended my career, but I got run over by a car."

She set down the broom she'd been using on the cobwebs and leaned against the wall. "I'm sorry, Bryan."

"Not as sorry as I was." He eased himself to sit on the edge of the table facing her, the toe of one worn work boot touching the floor. "I grew up playing hockey here for the Cowboys, but I was always better than the kids my age. When you're good at something like that, if you have parents like I did, they push you and you get extra training and better teams, better coaches, and then you get even better. It's like you have a spark and it gets fed and then the fire builds."

She nodded. She'd read about the compounding of advantage when practice and opportunity combined with talent.

"Really good kid hockey players go to play Juniors

in Canada." He had a screwdriver in his hand and he started flipping it lazily, catching it as it turned end to end. He looked up at her with a sideways grin. "I wasn't that good.

"Guys at my level, we play junior hockey here, a year or two before college, hoping for a scholarship, hoping to get drafted. I played for a team in Michigan. That's where I met Erin. I boarded with her family."

"Wait, you moved there? By yourself?"

"That's how it works."

She couldn't imagine that. What if Tim moved out? How had Bryan's mother let him go?

"Was your mom upset?"

He tossed the screwdriver again and caught it. "My mom? I don't think my family was much like yours. Besides, it was my big break."

His tone of voice tugged at her heart. It might have been his big break when it happened, but since then, his attitude had obviously changed.

"So you met Erin?"

"She was twenty, already working, I couldn't believe she was interested in me." He shrugged. "I was young and so stupid. Erin was older and good-looking. She didn't have to work hard to get into my pants. When I was drafted and had my college scholarship lined up, it looked like smooth sailing straight to the NHL. We got married and at the time, I thought it was my idea. Looking back, I guess Erin saw an opportunity to escape from her dead-end town and her dead-end job and she took it."

"Seriously?" Clare said. "You were married in college?"

"Before. The day I turned eighteen."

"I can't even imagine that." College for her had been confusing. She'd mourned Gretchen so long, but she'd also slowly awakened to the vibrant world around her on campus and in the dorms. She'd gone wild, taking advantage of her distance from home and her parents' increasing detachment. She couldn't remember saying no to anything—travel, parties, guys, whatever—until she'd found out she was pregnant and the reality of Tim crashed in on her.

"All I needed was a couple good years in college and then I'd be in the NHL. Erin and I were sure we had it made," he said. "You can't imagine how cocky I was. I had absolutely no understanding of how to care for what I'd been given." He flipped the tool again. "Right after my sophomore season ended, I was out with a bunch of guys from the team and we were messing around in a parking lot. Drunk. I was riding on the roof of one of the cars. My buddy didn't know I slipped off and he ended up dragging me. I don't remember it, but the other guys said he stopped when he finally heard me screaming."

"Bryan, that's horrible," Clare gasped.

"I'm telling you so you'll understand about Allie. She's the best thing in my life. The only really great thing. I learned from my screwup back then that I can't take anything for granted. Allie's having a tough time right now. She's not the easiest person to be around and she's upset. But she's a good kid and for some reason, she likes being near Tim. She doesn't deserve to get jerked around."

He stood up and came over to stand in front of her. "I know what you think about her. You don't trust her. But she's not a bully. You have to see that."

She wasn't sure what Allie was. She'd seen that fight

in the lobby, and the anger and viciousness had shocked her. Since then, though, the Allie who'd been in the mediation sessions was different. Sullen maybe, quiet definitely, but not violent.

"I'm not out to get her, Bryan."

"I hope not."

"You're a good dad," she whispered.

"I'm not," he said. "But I'm going to get there."

She shivered. All her life she'd wished for what Allie had. Bryan was on her side, one hundred percent, no questions asked. Or even better, all questions asked. His daughter had problems but he was standing right there, ready to take them on with her. He saw who she was and he loved her anyway.

Clare couldn't imagine what that would feel like. To be as open, as broken, as angry, as real as you were in front of another person and they'd still love you.

She wanted to touch him. Wanted him to touch her. He was so close that she could see every breath he took, could see the faint sheen of sweat in the hollow at the base of his neck.

He held still, watching her. She wondered what he saw.

"Why did you want me to put the tool belt on?" he asked, his voice low and sexy.

"Because," she said. "I…" But she couldn't finish her thought. Couldn't think anything at all. She didn't want to think anymore. She put her hands on the wide leather belt, felt the strength in his body as she tugged and he stepped closer to her. She lifted her face and he lowered his mouth and they kissed.

It was slow at first, as if he wasn't sure what he was doing or hadn't done it in a long time. But she wrapped her arms around him, pulling herself even closer and the extra contact, her breasts on his chest, touching at stomach, hip, thighs, was enough to push them on. She opened her mouth, demanding more, and he delivered, his hands roaming from her hair to her shoulders to her face.

He tugged on the ends of her hair and she tipped her head back. He took a strand of hair in his hand, running his fingers from the top of her head to the ends. His eyes tracked the movement and then he lowered his mouth to hers, whispering, "Beautiful," before pressing a kiss on her lips.

She didn't want the kiss to end, but he pulled back. His eyes were such a deep, dark blue. His hands were on her waist now, fingers spread as he held her close.

"Clare," he said. "God. I—"

He tightened his hands and pulled her closer. She could feel his erection through his jeans and it made her hot and eager. They kissed again, no hesitation this time, just a wild pull and hunger that left them panting. She tugged his shirt out of his jeans and got her hands up underneath, palms moving over the tight muscles in his stomach, along his waist, up his back. He groaned and pressed against her.

He leaned his forehead on hers before pulling back, taking her hands from his shoulders, pressing them in both of his own. He stepped away.

"I can't do this with you," he said. He lifted their hands and kissed hers. "Not because I don't want to, because, Clare, stopping now is one of the hardest things I've ever done."

"So don't stop," she whispered, giving him an encouraging, hopeful tug toward her. He didn't budge.

"I've never been with anyone but Erin. I told you how that started—it was physical. Just like this. I'm not choosing that road again. There's got to be more for me than the fact that I can't keep my hands off you."

"I can't keep my hands off you, either," she said, hating the defeated look on his face.

He smiled. "I wish that was enough, but it's not. You have all these walls up, Clare, and you're not planning to let me past any of them. You don't want me."

He let her hands go and moved his own back to her shoulders. He bent slowly, deliberately toward her. She stood on tiptoe and pulled his head until his lips met hers, shoving her hands into the soft waves at the back of his neck. He moaned low in his throat and kissed her so hard and so thoroughly her legs trembled.

She wanted more of him, more touching, more kissing, more of everything he had to offer, but that terrified her. She pulled him closer, hoping she could stop thinking and let him take her away.

He inched back, putting space between them again. "I love this, Clare. But it's got to be about more than how I feel when I'm kissing you."

A loud crash and then Allie's raised voice came from the other room.

She pushed Bryan away hard, yelling for Tim as she did. The two of them ran for the door and rushed out to the lobby. The kids were on the floor and all she could see was Allie on top of Tim and the two of them were rolling around in a mess of hockey sticks and plastic chairs. She yelled, "Get off him!" as Bryan pushed past her to grab his daughter by the arm.

BRYAN HADN'T SEEN the first fight and now, when he saw the kids rolling on the floor, he felt so sick, he was glad he'd been late that night. He pulled Allie up and held her while he tried to catch his breath.

Clare yanked a chair aside and then sat back on her heels when Tim struggled up from the floor. "Did she hurt you?"

Bryan's stomach sank. Allie made a soft sound but when he looked at her, she had her head down, staring at the floor. He put his arm around her shoulders.

"We weren't fighting. God, Mom. Get off me."

Tim brushed off Clare's hands and got to his feet. "Allie, are you okay?"

She nodded.

He didn't look at his mom as he said to Bryan, "I bought a bouncy ball from the machine and it got stuck on top of the light fixture. I put the chair up on the table and climbed up and I was sort of jabbing with the hockey stick, but then I lost my balance and the whole stack came down, me included, right on Allie."

"It was my fault," she said. "I was supposed to be holding the chair steady."

"You told me not to stand on the chair. You called me an idiot when I wouldn't get down." He glared at his mom. "But in a nice way. Because she didn't want me to get hurt."

Clare had struggled to her feet by then. She looked mortified, Bryan gave her that much credit, as she said to Allie, "I'm sorry I jumped to the conclusion that you were fighting."

The apology hung there for a second, awkward and unanswered. Allie shrugged. "It's okay."

"No, it's not," Clare said, surprising him. "Tim won't tell me exactly what happened between the two of you, but I was wrong right from the start to put all the blame on you. I am really sorry I jumped on you. I won't do it again."

Allie's arm crept up and went around his waist. She twisted her fingers in his T-shirt and he tightened his arm on her shoulders to reassure her.

"Thank you," Allie said. She lifted her head and met Clare's eyes.

Clare nodded.

"We should clean this mess up," Bryan said. "You guys can go if you want. Allie and I can finish."

He was surprised when Allie protested. "We're supposed to work together, Dad. Lila said no separate shifts."

He didn't see a way around it. "You're the boss."

It only took a few minutes for them to straighten up the lobby. Tim found the bouncy ball and started to toss it but Clare said, "Tim!" in a tone that made the kid stuff the toy back in his jacket fast.

He went back to the storage area to pick up his tools and lock the door for the night. When he was unbuckling the tool belt, he remembered how Clare had pulled on it, dragging him closer so he couldn't have said no even if he'd wanted to.

She poked her head around the door. "We're heading out." Their eyes met and he dropped the belt on top of the tool box. She glanced at her watch. He'd never noticed before that it had a completely blank face with small gold hands on a white background. How perfectly fitting that she wouldn't have numbers on her watch. Everything about her was so locked down, she wouldn't even give away the time.

"I hope she believed me," she said.

"She'll want to believe you."

"I'm sorry to you, too," Clare said. "I should never have gone along with the mediation because you're right, it's not fair to foster their friendship when we're leaving."

"That's one thing that's not fair," he said.

"What?"

"Nothing. I'll see you around, Clare." He bent to pick up the tool box and when he turned back to the door, she was gone. He couldn't explain to her that he wanted her to make an effort. He knew about being stuck in a job and if her work forced her to move, he would understand. What he couldn't accept was that she wouldn't even consider testing the waters. She was attracted to him and he obviously returned her interest. Allie and Tim were good for each other. He told Clare things he didn't normally tell anyone. She was on his mind all day. He made up excuses to talk to her, and looked forward to cleaning out this storage room with her as if it had been a lottery prize package.

None of that mattered to Clare. She didn't need him any more than Erin ever had. Less, even, since Clare didn't even need his paycheck. She'd mess around with him, probably even sleep with him, but she was determined to leave and nothing he or Allie or Tim had to say was going to tempt her to even hesitate over that decision.

THE COLD SETTLED IN deeper than ever the next week. Bryan wasn't sure how many kids would be at the Thursday night practice. A lot of families had a four-wheel-drive vehicle, but the snow was coming down hard when he called Allie to get her coat on.

He opened the front door to check the roads one more time.

"You sure you want to go?" he asked.

"Why?" Allie was bent over, digging her gloves out from under her backpack, which she'd dropped when she got in from school.

"It's snowing hard," he said. "Maybe you want a break?"

She looked insulted. "I never want a break. If Mom was still here, I'd be on the select team and I'd get to play six times a week. That's what I want."

"I'm sorry that didn't work out," he said. "Next year, I hope."

"Next year I'll probably be in California."

She opened the door and dragged her bag out. He flicked the lights off and followed her. She was probably right. They hadn't talked about it, but he didn't believe Erin was coming home.

The anticipation of losing her left a pit in his stomach. After the mess he'd made of things these past few weeks, he was sure Allie would want to go with Erin. Would Erin want her? He couldn't imagine that she wouldn't. Unless Lush scored another tour, but the chances of that weren't great. By this time next year, their family would be unrecognizable, he bet.

The roads were bad, but they made it to the rink. He hoped the plows would be out during practice or else driving home was going to be dicey. He scanned the lot for Allie's little Prius but didn't see it. He certainly hoped she'd had the sense to stay home. That car had no business on the road in an upstate winter.

His phone rang and he told Allie he'd meet her inside.

She got her bag and trudged up the stairs to the rink while he picked up the call.

"Bryan, it's Stan Meecham."

"Hey, man, it's good to hear from you."

Stan was the director of sales for Dutton Skates. He'd hired Bryan thirteen years ago and they'd become decent friends, meeting each year at the sales meetings and on a few corporate trips. "What's up?"

"I'm going to start by saying I'm not happy about making this call. I've put it off as long as I could, but even though we're friends, business is business."

Bryan's mind went blank for a second before he rallied. He called up his sales voice, the one he used when he was refusing to admit to hunger, tiredness or that a close on a sale was slipping away. "Don't sweat it, Stan. What's on your mind?"

"Your numbers are down, Bryan. You've lost a couple accounts and we've had calls from a couple more that you're rescheduling or cutting back on appointments."

"It's been rough," Bryan said. "I did have to cut back the travel schedule, but I'm getting the kinks worked out. Once the customers get used to the new routine, even with less face-to-face time, we'll be stronger than ever."

"You're under strain, Bryan, with your ex out of town, but it's unreasonable to expect that our clients are going to get used to a routine where they have a lower standard of customer service than Dutton would ordinarily provide."

Damn. Stan sounded pissed. He must have been sitting on this call for a while, building up a head of steam.

"Okay. So, what are you saying?" Bryan managed to

keep his voice steady even though he was gripping the phone tight enough to cramp his hand.

"There are three things that can happen. One, you go back to the previous schedule and improve the contact you have with the client accounts. Two, we reduce your territory, but that won't work because you don't have enough volume up there to support two guys. Or three, well, I'm not ready to talk about three, but you should know it's come up in the management meetings."

They'd talked about letting him go. It had already come up. He knew his numbers were down and that he'd lost three stores, but he'd figured he had time to get it under control.

It looked now as if he didn't have any time, and he didn't have a choice. Of the options Stan had laid out, losing territory or being fired were absolutely out of the question. That left only number one. He needed to go back to his usual travel schedule. Somehow, he had to make that work.

"I appreciate the call, Stan. I heard what you're telling me and I'm on it."

"We'd hate to lose you, Bryan. You know we took you on at first because Danny asked and we figured you could trade on your name for a year or two. But you've turned into one of our most reliable guys. If you can fix this, we're looking forward to a lot more years together."

"Consider it done," he said. They hung up. He stared into the parking lot where the snow swirled white under the streetlights and the rest of the land stretched out black and empty. What would it feel like to walk away and let himself get lost in that frozen night? He could let all his bad decisions fall behind him and stop worrying.

Headlights cut across his windshield as Clare pulled her car into a spot near the building. She was bundled up in a quilted ski jacket with her scarf hiding most of her face. Tim scrambled out and dragged his bag inside.

He'd told her the truth the other day. He and Erin had gotten together too young, too fast, and his life had been shaped by decisions he'd made when he didn't have a lot of alternatives. He felt the same pressure now. He wanted time. Time for Allie, to figure out how to balance her and his job so if Erin tried to take her to California, he could put up a fight. He wanted time to get to know Clare, to persuade her that he was worth a risk, to show her that he could be more for her than a physical thrill.

He slammed his closed fist on the steering wheel. Just like all those years ago, he wasn't going to get the time he needed to shape his choices.

CHAPTER ELEVEN

CLARE WASN'T A BIG FAN of hunting, but here she was, shivering and annoyed in the rink in Twin Falls, New York, with a trap baited and waiting. All she needed now was her prey. She moved the thermos of coffee an inch closer to the bakery bag of warm brownies. Lindsey had said all men respond to food. She hoped Bryan did because she needed to lure him into sitting with her long enough for her to apologize.

She was mortified that she'd jumped all over Allie. Tim hadn't talked to her for two days. Even after he'd broken down and asked her if she'd seen his iPod, things between them were more strained than ever. She hoped Bryan's daughter hadn't been too upset. She had seen signs of progress in Allie's confidence and she didn't want to set her back.

She wanted to apologize to Bryan about more than Allie, though. He was right when he said she wasn't willing to open up to him. She couldn't. Not to him, of all people. If only he knew how little she'd cared about any of the guys she'd dated over the years, that he was already more important to her than any of them had been. She wasn't shutting him out because she didn't like him, she liked him too much to let him get any closer.

So she needed to apologize and make sure Bryan understood she was going to stick with her own boundaries from now on. She wouldn't cross the line and confuse him again. She didn't want him hurt.

She put her hand on the outside of the bag. It was losing heat, but he had to come in soon. She'd asked a few subtle questions when she saw Mary at the school pickup line. Bryan was in town.

The kids were already on the ice. She scanned the nearly empty stands again. Maybe he'd gone to run an errand or something. She pulled out her book and started to read. She hoped the brownies would work even if they weren't warm when he finally got here.

BY THE TIME HE MADE IT into the rink after hanging up with Stan, practice was well under way. As he'd suspected, a lot of kids were missing—besides Allie and Tim, there were only about seven other skaters. Unsettled by his conversation with Stan, Bryan couldn't sit in the stands near Clare. He'd only seen three other parents in the lobby—people must have carpooled tonight. The skate shop was still closed, making it seem even more desolate. Danny had told him Nate Grimes didn't want to renew his lease on the place. They were looking for a new tenant, but for now, it was closed.

He paced the hallway that led from the back side of the ice to the locker rooms, keeping half an eye on the kids. How the hell was he going to keep up with Allie while he put his travel schedule back together?

Hugh Jeffries, the head coach, had the kids near the net on the end of the ice closest to him doing a shooting drill. He was about to start back down the hallway when he heard a commotion on the ice and saw one of the players throw his stick down. It wasn't Allie, he knew that because she was skating over from the opposite corner of the ice toward the kid.

Hugh was gesturing at the net and yelling something, but Bryan couldn't tell what. The kid who was causing the trouble took off his gloves and whipped them down and then skated off the ice. Allie started after him, but Hugh called her back.

It was Tim, he realized. Bryan was too shocked to move aside fast enough and Tim stormed right up to him. He was crying, Bryan saw, and he looked furious.

"Whoa there, buddy, where are you going?"

Tim tried to skirt around him, but Bryan planted himself in the way and reached for the boy's shoulders.

"I'm going home," Tim said.

"Practice isn't over yet, is it?"

"I'm done with hockey," Tim said. "I suck at it and it's stupid." He tried to jerk out of Bryan's hold, but he didn't manage to get free.

"Wait a second. You want me to get your mom?"

Tim looked at the stands where Clare was absorbed in her book. "No." He twisted with enough force to get out of Bryan's grip and head down the hallway.

Bryan waved his arms in the direction of the stands, but Clare didn't look up. Tim kicked the wall near the locker room door and Bryan made up his mind. He followed Tim. He hoped Clare might realize Tim was gone and come after him.

"Hey, slow down," Bryan said. "What happened?"

"Coach wants us each to make three shots in a row before we can move on to the next drill. Everyone is finished except me because I can't even make one shot in a row. They've been standing there for like fifteen minutes while I shoot the stupid puck over and over and it doesn't go in! I suck and I can't get better no matter how much I try!"

He was still yelling, but Bryan could see the anger cool into sadness. Clare wasn't coming. He really wasn't sure what to say to Tim, but he couldn't let him walk away. He put an arm across the boy's shoulders and steered him into the locker room.

"You haven't been playing that long. You need to practice some more, you know?"

"What's the point? My mom is making us move again and who knows if there will even be a hockey team where we go. Next school I go to, everyone will probably play polo or something and I'll suck at that, too. I can never, ever catch up."

When he sat next to Tim, the bench rocked back and then settled. The boy stretched his skates out in front of him and rubbed his hands down his cheeks to wipe away the tears.

"I'm not crying," he muttered.

"Nobody said you were." Then he asked, "Is that why you're playing hockey? Because it's popular here?"

"That's why I started. To fit in."

"So if you move to this school where the kids play polo, you'll do that to fit in? You won't miss hockey?"

Tim shrugged. He knocked his skate blade on the floor to dislodge a piece of ice.

"I'll miss it. Hockey is freaking awesome. But that's how my life works. I start stuff and we move." He kicked his skate harder on the floor. "I'm sick of it. I'm done trying."

Bryan had reacted instinctively when Tim came off the ice so upset. He would have reached out to any child in that situation. Now he was torn. He'd told Clare he would back off, wouldn't give Tim any extra attention, but the boy was miserable. Shouldn't he try to help? Especially when the help Tim needed was the only thing he'd ever really been good at?

"You want to sit here and get yourself together for a minute while I grab my skates?"

"I'm going home," Tim said, defeated.

"If you show me your shot, I guarantee I can help you out." He waited until Tim looked up. "If I give you a lesson and you still can't hit the net, then you quit."

"You're going to coach me?" Tim asked slowly. "Allie said you never coach."

"It's not coaching, just helping out a friend," Bryan said. Clare would have to understand. Stepping in was the decent thing to do, but more than that, whether she'd wanted it or not, he cared about this kid.

CLARE HAD BEEN sucked into the climax of the thriller she was reading and hadn't noticed the time passing. She looked up every once in a while, but Bryan never appeared in the stands. She didn't realize he was on the ice until practice was almost over. She noticed Tim first, at one end of the ice by himself, shooting pucks at the goal. At first she wondered if he was being punished for something but then she saw that a coach was there with him, helping him adjust his stance and his hand position after every few shots. Something about the coach's shoulders caught her eye and when she looked closer, she realized it was Bryan.

He skated to the middle of the ice and she was fascinated to see how easily he moved and how deftly he used his stick to corral pucks. Even if she hadn't watched those videos of him playing, she'd have been able to pick out the one person on the ice who really knew what he was doing. She wondered what it would be like to see him go all-out.

He kept her son at work passing and shooting. She watched Tim respond to the coaching. Even though she couldn't see their faces, the high fives and fist bumps made it obvious that the two of them were having a great time.

Clare ate one of the brownies and drank most of the coffee while Bryan demonstrated something having to do with passing and the net. Then she accidentally on purpose left the cap off the thermos so the rest of the coffee would grow cold.

She'd intended to apologize to Bryan but instead she was so jealous and angry she felt as if she was back in seventh grade watching Lindsey sending notes to Gene Fisk.

It wasn't fair that not only did Tim insist on playing this sport she didn't like, didn't understand and didn't want him to play, but now she had to watch him connecting with Bryan, of all people. She'd told Bryan to back off. She'd explained why it was important that he shouldn't feed Tim's fascination with him, and here she sat, watching Bryan help Tim build a life here without her.

She ate the other brownie, but couldn't taste a thing.

WHEN PRACTICE ENDED, Allie skated to the box and off the ice without a look. Tim seemed interested in hanging around to talk, but Bryan sent him in to change. He gave Hugh a brief report on what he'd seen, mentioning Tim's strengths and laying out some points he'd have to keep working on. The kid was a quick study, and because he was already a good skater, he could use more of his concentration for learning positioning and stick work.

"He's going to be fine," Bryan said.

"Maybe if he got some more one-on-one coaching he'd be better than fine," Hugh answered.

"I was helping, not coaching."

Hugh picked up his bucket of pucks and grabbed a forgotten water bottle from the wall of the players' box. "I guess I can't figure out why you don't coach. Allie is a great player. Didn't you ever want to get in there and help direct her career?"

"Why? So her career could turn out like mine?"

"Hell, yeah. Every guy in the adult league would kill to have had your career." Hugh started toward the locker room. "Thanks for stepping in with Tim. I was out of ideas."

Bryan watched the Zamboni pull out. He'd always loved watching the big machine groom the ice, sweeping away all the cuts and marks of a game and leaving it as good as new. Being out there with Tim hadn't felt like he'd expected it to. He'd never tried to coach because he'd been sure his competitive drive would overcome him and he'd strong-arm the kids, but when he'd been working with Tim, he'd felt calm. Competent. Content. He turned toward the locker room to take his skates off.

He sat on the bench next to Cody MacAvoy. Allie must have gone into the bathroom already to change. He was only half listening to the boys teasing each other. He wanted to get his boots on so he could duck out before Tim and avoid Clare.

"Thank a lot, Mr. James." Tim shoved Cody over so

he could sit down on the bench. His hair, which normally hung down in his eyes in that style that seemed to be so popular at the middle school, was wet and sticking up in front. His face was flushed and he smelled a lot like a kid who'd just played hockey for an hour. No sign of tears.

It felt good to see the kid recovered. Good to know he'd made a difference.

Bryan winked at him as he picked up a skate guard from the floor and put it on his right skate. "It's no big deal," he said.

"No big deal? Did you see my shot? I'm definitely going to score this weekend," Tim replied. "If you were the coach, we'd all be so awesome. How come you're not the coach?"

"I travel a lot." He had the guards on both skates now so he hooked his fingers in the laces and picked up his knee brace. "Remember those drills that we talked about. Every night. Get a rubber puck you can use at home in the basement or something."

"Yes, sir."

"That's my line, pal," Bryan answered. "And don't use the rubber puck in the living room. Moms hate that."

He left the locker room and checked the hallway for Allie. When he didn't see her, he debated whether to wait in the lobby or if he had less likelihood of running into Clare back here.

He didn't have a chance to make up his mind before she came around the corner. She'd traded her usual short, wool coat for a quilted jacket and while she was probably warmer, he missed that other coat. He couldn't see nearly as much of her in this new one.

She had a thermos tucked under one arm and a white

bakery bag in the other hand. She lifted the bag. "Do you like brownies?"

"Love them," he said. He hadn't had time to grab dinner before they came and he was starving.

"Me, too." She crumpled the bag and threw it in the garbage can outside the bathroom door. "I didn't realize coaching was another of your many talents."

She was definitely pissed.

"I wasn't coaching," Bryan said. "Tim was ready to quit. He came off the ice crying and I ran into him in the hall."

"He was crying?" Clare put her hands in the pockets of her jacket. "When?"

"You were reading. I tried to get your attention, but you didn't notice and I thought someone should talk to him."

"You could have come get me."

Bryan nodded. He kept his voice calm, but he was mad. This argument was so typical of Clare. Don't butt in. Don't get involved. She and Tim were a closed society and she didn't care who that hurt. "I could have. But what Tim needed was someone to show him how to get the puck off his stick into the net. Is that something you could help him with?"

"He's my son."

"So what? Should I have ignored him when he needed help?" Bryan asked.

"You're not his coach."

"You're right, I'm not a coach."

"That's what you always told me," Allie said. She must have come out of the bathroom when he was arguing with Clare. "But I guess it's different when it's Tim."

Perfect. Allie was pissed, too. Man, how many ways could a guy go wrong in one night?

"Allie, I wasn't coaching." He was getting tired of explaining this. "Tim was upset and I helped him out."

She and Clare both glared at him.

"Next time anyone needs my help, I'll be sure to say no," he said under his breath. "Let's go, Allie."

Right before they made it through the lobby doors, Tim came out of the locker room and yelled, "Thanks for all the tips, Coach James."

"I'm not a coach!" he said.

He could feel Allie's eyes roll even though she was three feet behind him.

It had stopped snowing and the parking lot was deep in the silence of a winter night after a big snowfall. He walked to his car and opened the trunk to put Allie's bag inside. He turned the engine on and told her to get in and get warmed up while he grabbed the brush from behind the seat.

The snow was heavy but wet, so it brushed easily off the windows. He wished it had been icy because he could have vented some of his frustration scraping. He finished his car and glanced back at the building. Clare and Tim still hadn't come out.

The wind cut across his face and he remembered how much she hated the cold.

He almost left, but he couldn't do it. Once he considered brushing her car off, he couldn't walk away and leave it. He was mad, not a jerk. He trudged across the lot and started on her back window.

When he finally slid behind the wheel of his Lexus, Allie was sprawled across the backseat. She sat up when he got in and they both pulled their seat belts on.

"How come you're back there, Allie? Making me play chauffeur?"

She didn't answer. He looked in the rearview mirror as he was pulling out of his space and he caught a glimpse of her wiping her cheeks.

"Are you crying?" he asked.

"No." The stuffy, muffled tone of her voice directly contradicted her answer. What was with these kids and denying the obvious?

He stopped the car and put one arm over the backseat so he could see her. "What's wrong, kiddo?"

"Nothing. I bumped my ankle, but it's fine now." She pulled her headphones out and started to put them in.

"Aren't we finished with the whole pretending nothing's wrong routine? We were going to talk to each other," he said.

She blinked. Her hair, which seemed to be in a perpetual tangle, had fallen across her shoulder.

"Why would you help him?" she asked in a rush. "You never ever went on the ice for me, but he's only been here for half of a season and already you want to coach him. Why him?"

"Honey, you saw how frustrated Tim was. He said he wanted to quit. He needed some help. It wasn't about you."

"I know it's not about me. You won't coach *me*. But all Tim has to do is be *pathetic* and all of a sudden you're Coach James."

He tried to reach her knee, to feel some connection with her, but she jerked away from him.

"Can we please go home?" she asked.

"We can," Bryan said. "But I never meant to hurt you."

She pulled herself closer to the door. He backed the car out and started driving home. He had to take it easy because the roads were slick so the drive took longer than usual. He had time to think about Allie and what he wanted to tell her.

"You know, Allie, I always said I wouldn't coach because of my schedule. That was true, but it was also because of my dad. You never met him, but he was..." He didn't even know how to describe his dad to Allie. "Well, he was hard to please. He coached my team the first couple years I played and it seemed like all he did was yell at me. I know he wanted to help me become a better player and I guess part of why I got as far as I did was because of him."

He checked in the rearview mirror. She was listening.

"But I hated it. I never liked playing for him and the years he coached were the ones when I didn't have fun."

"Did he yell at everybody or just you?" Allie asked.

"Me. He didn't care about the other kids much." Bryan smiled. "It wasn't all bad. And I loved to play. I loved it the way you love it. Like it was the only thing I wanted to do."

He caught a glimpse of her smile in the dark of the backseat.

"But, anyway, I don't coach you because ever since you were little, I loved sharing hockey with you. You and your mom had so much you did together. She was around all the time and it seemed like there wasn't anything that you needed me for except hockey. I was the one who went to your games and knew your teams. It was our thing. If I coached you and it turned out to be like it was with my dad, all hypercompetitive and crazy, I'd have hated it. You'd have hated me. I couldn't risk that we'd lose the one connection we had."

"You wanted me to have fun and not be serious because I'm a girl."

"No, that's not it."

"If I was a boy would you have coached me?"

"No!" he said. "Where is that coming from?"

"Because if I was a boy, I'd fit in and it wouldn't always be weird and awkward."

"You're going to have to explain this, Allie. What?"

"If I was a boy I could get dressed with the team instead of in the bathroom. If I checked someone or scored a lot it would be because I'm good, not a freak. And I'd have short hair and I wouldn't get called names on the ice. Or at least not the names they call me now."

"Who calls you names?"

"Jack Langenforth. But Tim and Cody made him stop. The other teams. Like trash-talking, but they say different stuff to me because I'm a girl."

Bryan remembered the things he'd heard hockey players say in locker rooms when he was playing. He felt sick. "Bad stuff?"

"Just different." She paused. "If I was a boy no one would try to kiss me."

She was moving too quickly for him. "Someone tried to kiss you? On the ice?"

"At school."

The last puzzle piece fell into place. "I suppose when this person tried to kiss you, you punched him."

"He shouldn't have tried to kiss me. I didn't even know him back then."

"Did he try to kiss you at the rink? The night when I was late?"

Allie picked up the end of her braid and fiddled with it the way she did when she was nervous. "He told me I was pretty. He said we should go out because we both play hockey and he was going to be as good as me and we could be the king and queen of hockey and rule the school." She sounded more and more depressed. Bryan could imagine Tim trying to coerce Allie into his plan when he realized how important hockey was as he was trying to fit in.

"*That's* why you punched him?"

"He wouldn't stop talking about it. Dad, when he kept saying it, I got this feeling all over my body like I was going to burst into flames. I don't want to be the queen of anything or kiss anyone and I especially don't want to rule the school. I want to be Allie just like I've always been. I don't want anything to change."

"Okay," Bryan said. "I get that."

He did get it, especially the last part. Everything had changed this year for her and not many of the changes had been for the better. She had a right to her anger even if she was expressing it wrong.

He put the blinker on and turned onto their street. "Has Tim tried to kiss you recently?"

"No," Allie said. "He kind of forgot that he wanted to because we do other stuff together now."

He pulled the car into the driveway and cut the engine. He turned around so he could see her better.

"So you're friends?"

"Maybe. I'm not sure. He wants your autograph really bad. That might be why he hangs around with me."

"Want me to give him an autograph and we can see if he leaves you alone?"

She touched the ends of her hair to her lip. "Not yet, I guess."

So the mediation was working. Or something was working. Whatever it was, he had some hope that Allie was going to come through this experience with a new friend. Which was a picture-perfect example of a mixed blessing. Allie and Tim had both started this school year needing a friend. If Clare stuck to her plan, they were going to be right back to square one when the next year started. Bryan had to swallow twice before he spoke. "How about us? Are we doing okay?"

She looked out the window. "I still wish I could be a boy."

"I can't help you with that," he said. "But you could cut your hair."

"Mom likes it long."

Mom's not in charge, he wanted to say.

"Allie." He waited until she made eye contact. "Mom would absolutely understand if you want to cut your hair."

"Okay," Allie said after a moment. "Can I go in now?"

"I guess," he said. "Leave your bag, I'll get it."

She opened the car door but paused before she got out. "Even though you know everything about hockey and are totally great, you don't make me feel stupid when I make mistakes on the ice. Tim sucks and you didn't yell at him. He actually looked kind of good by the end tonight." She turned her head so she could face him. "You shouldn't worry that hockey wouldn't be fun. Like what you said about your dad. You'd be awesome. If you ever did want to coach me, it would be okay even if you are the only one who ever benched me."

God.

She trusted him. He'd been worse than Clare all these years, trying to run guardrails around the time he spent with Allie. Why shouldn't he give her everything she asked him to give? How long was he going to hold back for fear he'd screw up?

"Get back in the car."

"What?"

"Get back in the car. Put your seat belt on."

"Why? Are we out of cereal again?"

"When you rush the puck and you get into traffic, you always look right first. You've got to be able to move both ways without missing a beat. If we work on that, if we get you comfortable going right or left, you're going to have more options in those situations."

She was still halfway out of the car.

"Come on, Allie. Let's go skate."

"You and me?"

"Yeah."

She shut the door and he backed the car out of the driveway. This was so not the best night for this. The roads were still bad and he would have to call Danny to meet him with a key. They actually *were* out of cereal again so they'd either have to stop on the way home or get up early enough for a quick run to the diner before school. On the other hand, he'd waited thirteen years to be the dad he wanted to be. Waiting another night wasn't something he was prepared to do.

"I can't get certified for a coach's card until next

year," he said quietly. "But we can try this, okay? Working together. We'll see how it goes. You tell me if you want me to back off."

"Thanks, Dad," Allie said. He heard her seat belt click open and he was about to tell her to put it back on when she scrambled between the seats to plop down next to him. "You need to show Tim how to deke. He *really* sucks at that."

Bryan had to smile. She delivered that criticism in the most cheerful tone he'd heard from her in months. Maybe Tim was merely a temporary friend and this time next year he was going to be tacking up polo ponies, but he wasn't leaving Twin Falls before he was a whole lot better at hockey. Not if Allie had anything to say about it.

CHAPTER TWELVE

PORK CHOPS, NOODLES, apple sauce, fresh green beans and a very small carton of chocolate-chip mint ice cream. All she needed now was milk and she could leave the grocery store for home. It had been three days since she fought with Bryan and she was still unsettled. She wanted to be out of the cold and inside her house where she could, maybe finally, get a good night's sleep.

The store was crowded—five o'clock was absolutely the wrong time of day to be in here—but she'd had a meeting that ran long in the morning, throwing off her schedule for the entire day. The toiletries aisle was mostly clear of other shoppers so she turned down it, hoping to reach the dairy case without encountering more crowds.

She pushed her cart quickly, reviewing the things she needed to do before she could crawl into bed. Tim needed a permission slip for a field trip with his science class and she needed to remember to wash her white blouse so she could wear it to a presentation she was making. She should probably make a haircut appointment for herself as well and then see about tickets to Seattle for the holidays.

She pushed her cart past the man standing in front of the feminine supplies but then something clicked and she turned back. "Bryan?"

He jumped, dropping the box of tampons he'd been holding. "Clare, I—" He leaned down to retrieve the box and tossed it into his cart.

His cart held one of just about every tampon and pad option the store carried. She stared at the heap for a second. "Opening a store?"

He rubbed his hand across his forehead. "Allie got her…um…her period. She's at home."

Clare nodded slowly. If she spooked him, who knew what else he might add to his cart. One of those horrid feminine deodorants, maybe.

She should keep going, grab her milk and go home, but she couldn't leave him. Judging from his body language, Bryan wasn't just embarrassed, he was terrified.

"It's her first time?"

He nodded. "I tried to call Erin but of course it's sound-check time or travel time or who knows what time on the tour so she's not picking up. Mary's youngest has the flu and when I called, Lisa said she was changing the sheets again." He pulled another package of pads off the shelf and squinted at the text. "Allie has cramps that hurt. Is it supposed to hurt?"

Clare reached for the package in his hand. "Let me see what you've got here, okay?"

He pointed at the shelves. "She made me a list, but the words on the list don't match the packages." He sounded as if he was taking the nonstandard labeling of the feminine-care industry as a serious quality-control failure. "What the hell is this thing where some of them have 'wings'? Is that a good thing? She didn't write wings, but maybe she should have them. Would she know about wings?"

"Let me see the list."

He handed it over and then put his hands in the front pockets of his jeans. He was wearing the same gray sweater he'd had on the night she met him. He looked upset and slightly pissed and totally adorable.

She straightened the list out and studied it. It was written on purple notebook paper in Allie's girlish script.

"You know," he said, "in the hardware store, they put the screws and nails together by type and then by size. You can find exactly what you need and not have to mess with all these options. The screws and nails make sense."

"Let me get this out of our way so we can see what's what," she said as she pushed his cart a few feet down the aisle. She didn't have the time and he didn't have the patience to reshelve all those things.

"This entire aisle should be rethought," he continued. "Preferably by someone who is capable of saying what they mean."

"Maybe by a man?" she murmured as she pulled a package of pads and one of tampons off the shelf.

"Ha. I know better than to agree to that."

She put the packages in the front basket of her cart and started off down the aisle. "Come on then. You have ibuprofen, right? She might feel like lying down. We should get her some magazines."

He started to reach for his cart, but she said, "Leave that. Someone will take care of it."

"Okay." He fell into step next to her, peering at the two packages. "You're sure that's all she needs?"

"Definitely."

She grabbed her milk and the two of them headed for the checkout. At the magazine rack, he picked out *Hockey Digest* and she added *People*. He asked her to wait while he bent down to study the lower racks and then straightened up, holding a photography magazine. "Good call," she said.

As they were running their things through the self-checkout, Bryan cleared his throat. "Thanks, Clare. I was losing it."

"It's not a problem. The first time doing anything with a kid can be upsetting."

"You're kind of amazing, though. You always know what to do."

She shook her head as she processed her credit card. "Not always, Bryan. Please."

"Seems that way to me."

He picked up his bag and waited for her to grab hers. "Listen, I'm really out of my depth here. I mean, when she said it hurts, I had no idea. Is that normal?"

"Unfortunately. Being a girl sucks."

They maneuvered through the crowds and out to the parking lot. An icy puddle of slush had formed next to the curb and they had to step carefully over it. Her heel caught a slippery spot and she skidded. Bryan's hand was under her elbow, steadying her, while she got her feet back under her.

"Okay?"

"Thanks," she said, aware that he was still holding her arm and surprised by how much she wanted to lean into his strength.

His car was parked near the cart return. He took his hand off her arm to dig in his pocket for his keys.

"Is she going to know how to work this stuff?" he asked.

Clare had a sudden memory of her and Gretchen stealing their mother's tampons and giggling over the instructions on the box. The day she got her first period, she'd felt so miserable and her mom had been no help. Eventually, she crawled into her sister's bed and they'd read back issues of *Seventeen,* trying to figure out how much of what she felt was normal. Standing in the cold, damp, upstate New York evening, Clare was sure she could smell her sister's shampoo and feel the sun that had streamed into Gretchen's bedroom that day.

She shivered.

Allie was home alone waiting for her mom to call from three-thousand miles away. Would she be able to ask Bryan her questions? The James family didn't have the most impressive communication skills on a good day.

"Clare?" he prompted. She realized she hadn't answered him.

"She'll be fine."

"I guess. I wish Erin would call back." Bryan looked worried. "Clare? I know I shouldn't ask."

Please don't say it, please don't say it.

"I don't suppose there's any chance you'd come by and talk to her?"

"No," she said desperately. "Please. I can't."

"What's wrong?" He must have heard the emotion in her voice. If she didn't pull it together, he was going to ask her more questions and she was close enough to crying that she just might break down and tell him about Gretchen. Then she might find herself at his house, talking to his lonely daughter and trying to make him laugh. And then they'd be part of her and if anything happened to them, she wouldn't be able to take it. She couldn't.

"Sorry," she said. "I have to get home because I have a client call that I can't miss."

"Oh." He squinted at her. "Are you okay?"

"Yep," she said. "Just cold." Her car was a few rows over. "I'll see you."

She put her head down against the wind and started walking. She made it a few feet, but she kept seeing him as he was that first night, holding Allie's face, touching her because he didn't trust his eyes to tell him she was okay. She turned back. He was already pulling out of his space so she had to wave to get his attention. He rolled down the window.

"You don't need me. You were dealing with Allie before I showed up and when you get home you're going to be what she needs. Trust yourself."

He ducked his head but then met her eye. "Thanks."

"No problem," she answered. He drove away and she whispered, "Keep me posted."

This was all wrong. Wrong, wrong, wrong.

He was so hard to resist. He didn't even know how much it meant to her that he'd trust her to talk to Allie. What an amazing man, to be able to admit there were things he wasn't confident about and then to find someone he hoped would be able to give his daughter what he couldn't.

He'd offered her a gift, his trust and the opportunity to get to know his daughter better, and she'd turned him down. She hadn't shown up when he needed her, she hadn't even let him help when Tim needed him.

It was too much. Her memories of Gretchen and the enormous, unrelenting loss she still felt every day were too big and too painful. How could she possibly help Bryan's daughter when it would hurt just to look at her?

She wished she could go back to the first time Allie hit Tim. She'd pack him up and the two of them would move somewhere else and she would keep on with her small, safe existence. If only she'd been smart enough to run before she started losing her heart.

RIGHT AFTER THE FIASCO at the grocery store, Erin had called back. Lush's lead singer had come down with a sore throat and the tour was stalled. She made a reservation and flew in that night.

He let her and Allie have the apartment and he made a quick run to as many clients as he could fit into three days. He and Erin barely talked, but that hadn't been the point of the visit. She'd come to see Allie.

They dropped Erin off at the airport around five. On the drive home, Allie was quiet in the seat next to him. He turned on the radio and her top-forty station came on. He switched it to the far superior classic-rock station and she didn't seem to notice. She was probably upset. Saying goodbye to Erin again had to be hard. He switched back to the top-forty station and when she still didn't seem to notice, he turned the volume up. He'd give her time to adjust.

Back at the apartment, Bryan asked Allie if she wanted to order a pizza.

"You eat too much takeout," she said. "I'm making quesadillas."

"You're cooking?"

"I learned how in my Granny Skills class at school."

"Your what class?"

"Tim calls it that. The real name is Family Consumer

Science. We learned how to sew pillows out of felt, too, but that's not as useful as quesadillas."

"Do we even have the stuff to make quesadillas?" Bryan opened the refrigerator and looked in. He wasn't sure what exactly went into a quesadilla, but there was always a possibility he'd accidentally bought it. Not a big possibility, but since he seemed to unexpectedly run out of something every week, it stood to reason he might have also unexpectedly stocked up.

Allie shoved him out of the way with her hip. "We have the stuff. Mom took me shopping. But I'm cooking." She waved toward the living room. "You can go... do something."

She sounded confident, but still... "Are you sure you're old enough to use the stove?"

"Dad, I took a class." She pointed to the doorway. "I won't mess up."

He went into the living room and flipped on ESPN. His stomach had started to growl about fifteen minutes into the wait. He was hungry, but more than that, the quesadillas smelled good. He'd gotten so used to the stale smells of takeout that he couldn't remember the last time the apartment smelled like cooking. Maybe it never had.

She walked by the living-room doorway and he heard the front door open. When she passed again on her way back to the kitchen, she was carrying a ceramic Buffalo Sabres mug with a clump of holly she must have cut from the bush next to the steps.

They sat down at the round kitchen table. She'd put place mats out and real napkins he didn't even know they owned. The mug of holly was in the middle. When he picked his napkin up to put it on his lap, he saw a price sticker from their local grocery store and guessed Allie had bought them when she bought the food. She came to the table carrying two plates, each holding a quesadilla, two rings of canned pineapple and something he thought was coleslaw.

She sat with her hands in her lap, leaning over her plate, watching him intently. He dug in.

"This is fantastic, Allie," he said after he'd taken two huge bites. "Remind me to write a thank-you note to your Granny teacher." He wondered if she'd bought enough ingredients to make him another quesadilla or three. He wasn't sure he was going to try the coleslaw but he figured he could move it around enough to make it look as if he'd had some.

Allie hadn't started her meal.

"Aren't you hungry?" he asked around another mouthful.

"Mom's staying in California. She wants me to move there with her."

He felt as if he was going to choke. His mouth was dry and he suddenly lost interest in the food. He forced the bite down and then took a sip of his water.

"When?" he asked.

Allie hunched her shoulders and looked at him, her eyes wide and nervous in a way they hadn't been in a long time.

"June," she said. "But…"

She looked back down at her plate. She must be worried about starting at a new school, or moving across the country. That would be intimidating for anyone.

"June," he said, trying to force his voice to sound cheerful. "That'll give you time to meet some kids out there before school starts."

"Dad." Her voice cracked. "Aren't you even going to…"

"It'll be okay, Allie. Don't worry."

"No. It won't be okay." She pushed her chair away from the table and he braced himself. She took a deep breath and said to herself, "You can do this." He watched her relax her shoulders and lay her hands flat on the table. She took another steadying breath and then said, "I want to stay with you."

"You what?"

"I'm not the same as I was before when I lived with Mom. When she was here this weekend, it was like I was a little kid again. She doesn't talk to me the way you do. You wait to hear my answers like they're interesting. Like they matter. We figure stuff out together, but Mom just tells me what to do." Allie paused. "I know it's probably not going to work because of your job, but I called Lila and she said I would never get anything I wanted if I didn't say I wanted it out loud. She said I had to be brave enough to ask." She hesitated. "So I'm asking."

"You want to live with me full-time?"

There were so many things he should be considering, but the only thing that mattered to him right then was Allie and the way she was nodding her head fast, then faster.

"I'll still miss her, but Mom's busy," she said. "And you know she doesn't love hockey like us."

He wished he knew if crying in front of your kid was damaging to their psychological development, but then he was glad he didn't know because he was crying in front of Allie and he couldn't make himself hide it.

"Nobody loves hockey like us. It's a sickness."

"I don't care."

He stood and opened his arms. "Come here, kiddo." She was out of her chair and had her arms around his waist before he could blink. She slammed into him hard enough to bump him against the table and his plate fell, shattering on the tile floor.

She stiffened, but he held her tighter and kissed the top of her head.

"I'm going to need a refill on the quesadillas," he said.

"We're learning chili next."

"If they have Advanced Granny Skills, make sure you sign up."

"Can I really stay, Dad?" Allie asked.

"We'll have to talk to your mom."

"She said it was up to me."

He had no idea how he was going to work this out. None. He'd find a way, though. His kid was asking to stay with him because this was where she wanted to grow up. With him. Damned if he was going to let her down now.

"Then, yeah. We're sticking together. Absolutely."

BRYAN WAITED UNTIL HE WAS sure Allie was asleep and then he set himself up with paper and pen at the kitchen table. He'd talked to Erin and they'd agreed that if he was keeping Allie full-time, he wouldn't have to send money anymore. She had a job offer lined up for after the tour and was feeling confident about her prospects.

He'd borrowed a tablet from Allie and at the top of one purple-lined sheet, he wrote down the dollar amount he needed to keep their family going. He carefully numbered the lines from one to twenty-five and then because he was too nervous to start filling in the list, he made a second column from twenty-six to fifty. No one could say he was lacking optimism.

Next to number one, he wrote gym teacher. It wasn't a real possibility because he hadn't finished college, but he had to start somewhere. When he was finished, he'd generated forty-two ideas and only three of them involved the fast-food industry. Four, if he counted delivering for Gusti's. He crossed off bartending (number twelve) and male escort (number twenty-nine) because he didn't want to *(a)* work at night or *(b)* introduce Allie to the escort industry.

He knew he should approach this systematically. He should categorize the viable choices, rank them, maybe make more lists, but he kept coming back to number eight. Skate school.

He circled it and then put the tablet down and went into the kitchen for a glass of water. He took a sip of water, dumped the rest down the drain and grabbed a beer out of the fridge. He drained half of it with one swallow and then drained the rest while he was dialing Danny's number.

He told Danny his plan and waited nervously for his friend's answer. He had to hold the phone away from his ear when Danny yelled, "Hell, yes, Bryan! It's about damn time."

It wasn't going to be that easy, of course. Danny suggested that he should take over the lease on the skate shop at the rink. He'd had an idea about some exclusive deals with Dutton, and Bryan made notes for a meeting he'd have to set up with Stan. He had to make schedules and plan rates, scare up some other coaches and see which of his buddies from his playing days would be willing to come back to guest coach during the camps he was planning for the school breaks. There'd be insurance and bank loans and a million other details.

There was a lot to do. Even as he flipped pages in Allie's notebook and wrote down the points he and Danny were generating, he couldn't help wishing he could call Clare. She'd make a joke about the idiocy of anyone planning to make a living out of hockey, but then she'd probably give him tips about business.

He wondered what would happen if he told her how often he thought of her and how much he wished he could spend more time with her. Could she change her mind about him and decide to stay? He'd never expected that Allie would choose to live with him—he'd been wrong about her. Could he be wrong about Clare? What if he just hadn't approached her the right way?

Then he remembered how she'd panicked in the parking lot. She'd said he wouldn't understand her life. That might be true, but he wished she could open up to him. Maybe whatever it was that scared her so much wouldn't be so terrible if they could face it together.

"THE SUPREME OVERLORDS have made a decision about the work today," Tim said.

Bryan dropped the load of tape and drop cloths he'd been carrying inside the door to the party room. They had planned to tape the room off today and paint the walls. Then they'd have one or two more sessions at most to finish the trim and hang the photo collage.

He and Clare had been friendly toward each other, but it was a false, excessively careful friendliness that was plain uncomfortable. He was getting really tired of it.

"What's the decision?" Clare asked.

He hadn't seen her since the afternoon at the grocery store last week when she'd saved him from bankrupting himself in the toiletries aisle. Her hair was tucked behind her ears and she was wearing a short-sleeved T-shirt with faded jeans. The hint of skin visible through the small rip on her thigh tantalized and distracted him.

"We've decided you and Mr. James should work here while Allie and I go on a pizza run."

"Don't be ridiculous," Clare said.

"It's not ridiculous, Mom, it's delegating."

"Well, I suggest you delegate yourself over near the windows. Start taping."

"Mom, that's not how this is supposed to work."

Bryan stepped forward. "I don't believe you guys are supposed to make us finish all the work, either. That's an abuse of power."

Tim shrugged. "We're powerful. We can't help it."

"We'll shoot you for it," Allie said.

"What?" Tim squeaked.

"Shut up. We'll totally win. They have my dad, but we have you *and* me."

Allie's confidence in him ended Tim's objections. "All righty, looks like we're having a shoot-out."

"Wait," Clare said. "I protest. We should all work together and get the room done."

"I'm down for the shoot-out," Bryan said. "We'll win and for once the Supreme Overlords will have to work while we loaf at the pizza place."

"I can't skate."

"We'll do it right here," Allie said.

"Bryan—"

"Clare." He smiled. "Trust me."

She gave in and he couldn't help feeling happy that for once, even in this small thing, they were on the same team.

"I CAN'T BELIEVE you cheated," Clare said as they settled into a booth in the back room of Gusti's Pizza.

"I did not cheat."

"You took advantage of your skills and beat children in a shoot-out so you wouldn't have to work."

"Did you see their faces when they realized they didn't have a chance?" Bryan shook his head. "I've watched every game Allie ever played *and* I taught Tim how to shoot. What made them dream they could take a shot I couldn't block?"

"That thing you did, when you picked the puck up on your stick and flipped it in over your shoulder. That looked more like lacrosse than hockey. When would you even learn something like that?"

"I guess the meaning of 'I grew up on the ice' is finally starting to sink in?" he said.

The low lighting and dark red leather booths in Gusti's were doing wonderful things for Bryan's skin and eyes. The lamp over their table cast shadows, but picked out the planes of his beautiful cheekbones.

She hadn't planned to be alone with him, and definitely would have preferred if they could have just finished the painting, but now that they were here, she was enjoying herself. He was so easy to be with. She relaxed into her seat, warm for what felt like the first time in months.

"You think they're working?"

"The Supreme Overlords? I doubt it." He leaned back in the booth and took a sip of his Coke. "Allie liked the magazines," he said. "Bet I'm going to find that photography one lying around with pages turned down right before Christmas."

"Tim does that with his video-game magazine."

"Thanks again for helping me out...with the shopping."

"Believe me, any woman would have taken pity on you."

"That's all it was, pity?"

She wanted to say it was. If only she could honestly say she'd seen a guy panicking and helped him out of pity.

"Not entirely," she admitted, and that was as far as she would go. "I care about you."

He gave her a look she couldn't interpret.

"Have you been on your own with Tim from the beginning? I mean, you said you were never married, but were you together with his dad at all?"

"Matteo and I went on a total of three dates. We met at a party. We went to another party. We saw a movie."

"You had a baby together."

"That's about it."

"He didn't stick around?"

"He was doing research at Stanford on a short-term visa. He was already back in Italy by the time I found out I was pregnant. Sticking around wasn't an option."

Bryan was silent for a few seconds. She straightened the salt and pepper shakers and then put them carefully in front of the container of parmesan cheese on the edge of the table.

"Wasn't an option for him or wasn't an option for you?"

"Bryan, what are you trying to find out? If I contemplated marriage to a guy I slept with twice, neither time very satisfactory since we were both trashed? Is that it?"

"I'm trying to figure out if you've ever let down your guard long enough to allow someone else in."

"That's ridiculous."

"Is it?"

She didn't tell people about Gretchen. It was easier for everyone if she kept her sister to herself, but he was looking at her as if he understood her and he couldn't possibly understand. Nobody could.

"I don't owe you an explanation of my choices."

"True, you don't owe me anything." Bryan reached for her hand. "But would you tell me anyway? You're leaving in a couple months, but you and Tim are always going to be part of my life. Part of a time when it changed for the good. I won't ever be able to unwind you and Tim from this year when Allie and I finally found each other. You're not someone I'm going to forget and I wish... well...I wish a lot of things, but above all I wish I understood why. It's hard to be with you, the way we are today, and to not understand why we can't try to stick this out."

She'd been prepared to argue with him. But then he held her hand and told her he would never forget her and she knew he meant it. She'd been pushing him away and he kept coming back. Because he cared.

It had been so long since she'd been with anyone who cared enough to protest when she shut the door. She'd perfected her defenses, gotten so good at picking partners who wouldn't have cared even if she'd asked them to, but somehow Bryan had found a weakness.

She smoothed her hand down the leather seat next to her. She'd tell him. He deserved an answer.

"My sister, Gretchen, is two years older than me. She died a few weeks after I went to college. We knew she was dying—knew it for ten years before it happened. More than half of my childhood was spent watching her lose ground every day. I grew up and she isn't here to share my life with me."

She brushed a hand across her eyes. Bryan's grip on her other hand tightened. She tried to smile at him but it didn't quite work and he stood up and then slid into her side of the booth. His hip bumped hers and his thigh was warm. She felt the solid warmth of his chest and shoulders. She could have that warmth if she leaned toward him. She kept herself carefully upright, but she didn't pull her hand away.

"Clare, I'm so sorry," he said.

"Shush. I'm telling you this once and then we're not going to talk about it again, so let me get through it."

He slid his arm around her shoulders. "Okay."

"Gretchen and I were close—more than close. We shared everything, even my experiences because hers got to be a nightmare and sometimes she needed to get out of herself, be away from herself. I was going to stay home and go to college in Seattle, but she made me leave. She called it Operation Fly the Coop. I'd barely settled in at Stanford when she died. I think..." She paused. She'd never told anyone else this, not even Lindsey. "I think she sensed she was dying and she wanted me out of the house. So I'd have the next stage of my life started and something to go back to after she died."

"Clare, I had no idea."

"No one does. No one has any idea what it felt like,

what it still feels like to live with the memories of watching her die. I never want to go through that again." She tightened her jaw and made sure her words came out strong. He had to believe her. "I never meant to get pregnant, had no intention of having a family, but I let my guard down. Tim came along and I couldn't not love him. He's my baby and always will be. But it's hard. For the past thirteen years, I've felt so exposed because I love him too much. I worry and I make bad decisions and I'm constantly trying to sift what's real and what's my screwed-up brain. It's better for everybody if I keep myself out of your life. Trust me. I'm not capable of normal."

Bryan tightened his arm on her shoulder.

"I don't know what I imagined you were going to tell me, but it wasn't this. I'm so sorry," he said.

"Can we not talk about it? It doesn't help."

Bryan patted her arm.

They sat silently in the booth while the business went on around them. The lunch crowd was gone and it was too early for dinner, but people came and went, the bell on the door tinkling, and the Gustis who were working the counter or waiting tables called out greetings. Twin Falls was a place people grew up in and didn't leave. She'd told Lindsey a long time ago that she didn't know why Tim would latch on to this town when they'd lived in so many more interesting places. She understood why now. Twin Falls was a place where you could belong.

"I don't talk about Gretchen," Clare said. "I told you because I didn't want you to feel it was you or Allie or anything else standing in our way. It's me. Just me."

The teenager behind the counter called Bryan's name. He hesitated and she gave him a shove. They were not going to dwell on this. She'd explained so he wouldn't imagine he could fix things between them or change her mind. But now that he had the facts, they weren't going to talk about it anymore.

He stood and held his hand out for hers. She shook her head. "Don't, Bryan. Don't be nice to me."

He took her hand and, God help her, she let him, his strong and gentle grip easing her from the booth, telling her he was there for her but he wasn't going to push for more than she could give.

A BREEZE BLEW UP and swirled snow around their boots as they went around the corner of the pizza place to the small lot where he'd parked his car. He put the pizza on the roof and the bag of sodas on the ground near his feet while he dug in his pockets for his keys.

"I don't know how you stand the weather," Clare said, forcing a casual tone. She was building her walls back up as fast and hard as she was able. "It's nasty without even really trying."

She had her new quilted jacket on again and a wool cap pulled down close to the tops of her glasses. He was used to her being in charge—she'd intimidated him at first. Right now she had tears in her eyes and, with her shoulders hunched against the cold and a smile that wasn't fooling either of them, she looked lost.

She'd been eighteen when her sister died, not much older than Allie. Ever since then, she'd been doing her level best to shut off her emotions, to protect herself from reliving the horror of losing the person she loved best. He guessed some people would find her cold, but he knew her. Only a person capable of loving utterly and completely would be so scared of loving again. She hadn't let go of her past and couldn't fully face the future.

When he lost his hockey career and his scholarship, he'd had a taste of the kind of anxiety she lived with. It broke his heart that Clare was going to move on again, taking her hurt and her love with her without anyone to lean on or to show her what it meant to be safe now, to be here now.

He'd assumed all along that she didn't want him.

He wished he could take away her fear and give her one moment of feeling cherished and safe and whole. Maybe she wouldn't let him, but he was going to try.

"There are ways to keep warm," he said. He moved around in front of her so she was between him and the car. His body was blocking some of the wind, but it was also, conveniently for him, positioning her right where he wanted her. "You just have to make the right moves."

"Bryan, don't make this harder than it already is," she said, but she didn't push him away. When she tilted her head back so she could see his eyes, she grabbed the sides of his jeans and pulled him close.

He bent his head and their lips met. He moved his hands so they were on either side of her head, pressing into the metal of the car, holding himself up because Clare was going to kill him. Her mouth opened and he kissed her, cupping the back of her head and then broke away to tug his gloves off. "I want to feel you. I love your hair," he said before going back to kissing her.

"I want you to feel me, Clare," he whispered as he pushed one leg between hers. "I want you to know I feel you. Right now." He lifted the edge of her hat and kissed the warm spot under her ear then nibbled down to her collar. "We're not thinking about tomorrow or next week, be here with me, right now."

She pushed her hands up between them, her fingers curled into fists on his chest. "There's no point, Bryan." She pressed against him, her mouth seeking his, laying more kisses on his lips, his jaw, his neck.

"The point is you," he said. "You. Just you. Let me love you right now. Let me be with you. Don't worry about what's next."

"I can't," she said, but she tugged the zipper of his jacket down and pushed her arms inside. "Please."

"Let me do this, Clare. Let me."

Her cheeks were cold when he touched them and she shivered.

"Wait," he said. He reached around her and opened the door to the backseat. "Get in."

She lowered herself to the seat, not letting go of his shirt. He gently untangled her hands, and then opened the driver's door, stuck the key in and turned the heat up. He slammed the front door and then bent to crawl in with her.

She stretched under him, her hands were inside his jacket again, wrapping around his torso to pull him to her. He knelt above her, his back to the door. His knee was killing him where it was wedged against the seat, but when he took in Clare's flushed skin and bright eyes, he forgot all about the pain. He kissed her forehead, her eyelids, her cheeks, her chin, her mouth.

She responded, tugging at his jacket until he twisted out of it. She ran her fingers in his hair and down inside the neck of his shirt, her touch on his skin so thrilling he drew in a breath.

"Too cold?" she asked.

"Exactly right," he answered. He cupped her breast through her sweater. She moaned and pushed up against him.

He tilted his head and kissed her neck again, drawing his lips down from a spot just under her ear to the hollow at the base of her throat. He loved the way her firm body felt under him. He loved the way she was responding to his touch with deeper moans and the way her mouth felt on his when he went back for more.

The windows fogged as she dragged his shirt free and stroked her hands down the front of his jeans. He couldn't move much, but he managed to spread her jacket, sliding it down one shoulder to her arm so he could feather kisses across her collarbone, tasting her and driving himself to want more.

He lost track of time, temperature—everything—as he loved Clare.

"Ow, wait. Stop, Bryan. I can't feel my legs." She pushed against his chest, but this wasn't the desperate-to-feel-you kind of pressure, this was get-off-me-you-big-lummox pressure. He twisted and lifted with a muffled groan and his knee let him know exactly how badly he was treating it. She managed to drag herself out from under him. He sat next to her, massaging his knee with his left hand as he put his right across her shoulders, slipping his hand under her jacket and wishing he could strip the rest of their clothes off.

"I have never regretted getting old as much as I do right at this moment," Bryan said. "If we were teenagers—"

"Backseats always seem bigger when people do this in the movies."

He drew her in close to hold her. She felt perfect right there.

"We need to go someplace, Clare. I can't take this. Where can we go to be alone?"

She twisted away from him.

"You said you knew we couldn't take our relationship any further."

"I did, but you feel what's between us the same as I do. Can't you trust me?"

"I can't trust me. Weren't you listening to anything I said?"

He hadn't really thought beyond wanting to give Clare a gift, to be with her in the moment and let her be with him.

Before he could formulate an answer, she opened the door and got in the front. He sat in silence looking at the back of her head while the motor ran.

Once he'd stowed the now cold pizza in the backseat and turned the car around to pull out of the lot, she was ready to talk.

"I didn't want to hurt you, Bryan."

"I'm not hurt," he lied. He drove on autopilot, not able to figure out how he'd gone from the high of having Clare in his arms to this frosty nothing with her next to him, but so far away. "I understand what you're feeling, but at the same time, I don't understand and never will."

THE DOOR TO THE party room was closed when they got back to the rink. Bryan was carrying the pizza and the bag with the soda, so Clare pushed the door open for him.

The kids had actually accomplished a lot, was Clare's first thought.

Oh, good Lord save us, was her second.

"Holy crap, Allie!" Bryan said. "What happened?"

"I told you I wanted to get my hair cut."

"Doesn't she look awesome?" Tim said, stepping over the piles of long dark hair at his feet to admire his handiwork.

Bryan put the food on the table and the two of them crossed to the center of the room where Allie was seated in one of the folding chairs, a clean drop cloth around her neck and covering her entire body. Tim, true to his nature, hadn't approached this task halfway. He'd given Allie a super-short style that left soft, wispy layers around her face.

He was right, Clare realized. Allie looked beautiful. The short layers brought out the slim planes of her face, accentuating her big eyes and the cheekbones she'd inherited from her dad. It wasn't a perfect cut—she could see from here that the left side was longer than the right over Allie's ears, and the top layer in the back was too short, but it was a vast improvement over her old, tangled length.

The only trouble was, an hour ago, Allie had had several feet of additional hair on her head and unless Clare missed her guess, neither the stylist nor the client had asked permission before making this change.

Bryan put one hand out and stroked Allie's hair softly.

"How does it look, Dad?"

"You didn't see it?"

"Tim wouldn't let me see."

"We didn't have a mirror," Tim protested.

Clare took out her phone. "You can take a picture."

Bryan took the phone and snapped a picture. He handed it to Allie who scowled.

"I told you I wanted it like a boy!"

"I cut it short. You want a buzz cut?"

"No," Clare and Bryan said at the same time.

"This is worse. Now I really look like a girl."

Tim was shuffling his feet.

"You're beautiful, Allie," Clare said. "You're not going to be mistaken for a boy any time soon, but that's not a bad thing. You're who you are." She'd captured the girl's attention. "You're a brave kid and you're playing boys hockey because you know what you want. Being thirteen is all about being the same as everybody else, so kids like you, who already know a little about what they want…well…it seems as if you don't fit in. But just wait, Allie. Just wait and you'll see how amazing you are."

"Ms. Sampson?" Allie said her name tentatively. Clare didn't think she'd ever said it before. "Thanks."

"Allie's had long hair forever," Tim said. "I gave her the first short haircut of her entire life. That's almost as big as, like, teaching her to ride a bike. She will never forget this moment."

Tim's words hit her hard. They were almost an exact echo of what Bryan had said at Gusti's. The four of them had changed each other. There was no removing the memories they were making now.

She couldn't stay here anymore. Couldn't be with these people who were insisting on breaking down her defenses when her defenses were the only way she stayed sane.

"Tim, we have to get home," she said.

"But, Mom, we still have work to do."

"Sorry, we can't finish today. Let's go."

Tim looked confused, but he crossed his arms. "I'm not going."

Bryan was behind her, but she didn't look at him, just grabbed her purse.

"I want to finish painting. We had a consensus!" Tim said.

"We can bring him home," Bryan told her quietly.

"But we're supposed to work together. You have to listen to us," Tim said.

"I'm leaving. If you want to stay, that's up to you."

He moved closer to Allie. "I'm staying."

Of course he was.

She turned on her heel and left them there. She was almost through the lobby when Bryan caught up to her.

"You're scared," he said. "I saw the second you flipped. It was when Tim mentioned the future. You keep moving and keep Tim moving so neither of you can ever really get to know anyone—you don't want to build anything that might break."

"Stop," Clare said. "Leave Tim out of it."

"But he's the point of it," Bryan said. "Isn't he? You've got him locked down so tight, he's going to have to pick between what he wants and you."

She closed her eyes as if he'd hit her. "You did not just say that to me."

"You're so scared to get close to anyone, you keep pushing away anyone who might love you."

She heard him say love. Another punch, this one in her stomach. She walked out. As she trudged to the car,

Clare felt colder than ever. She hated this place. Hated every cold, hard thing about it.

IT HAD BEEN MORE THAN a week since the fight at the rink and Clare still felt horrible. She'd been stewing about the things Bryan said and the things Tim wanted and she felt as if she was coming apart.

If they stayed here, Bryan wouldn't give up. He wanted to love her enough to heal her, but that wasn't possible. Knowing he cared made everything worse.

But he'd been right about Tim. She'd known it for a few months now and hadn't wanted to face it. If she didn't find a way to give him a permanent home, he was going to hate her.

She stopped in the door of Tim's room before he went to bed. "Tim? Can we talk?"

"I guess," he said. He was still mad at her.

"I spoke to Lindsey. She recommended me for a position with her company and I'm going to fly out for an interview next week. If everything goes well, when my contract is up, you and I can go back to Seattle and stay until you're finished high school. If this job doesn't come through, I can keep looking until I find something permanent, but as of now, it looks like this one is a go."

"Seattle?" Tim asked. "You're making me move to Seattle?"

"You told me months ago that you wanted to go back there."

"That was before. Mom, I live here now. I have my team and my friends. *This* is where I want to stay."

"But Seattle is where the house is. Lindsey's there. You can make friends there."

Tim jumped up from his bed, knocking over a pile of

books. "You don't get it, Mom. You can't just make new friends. Everyone in the world is not replaceable. These are my friends, Allie and Bryan and the guys from the team. I want these people."

"Well, I'm sorry, Tim, but I don't—"

"If you make me move, I'll run away," he said. His voice was shaking, but he wasn't shouting anymore. Instead, he sounded serious. Matter-of-fact. His hair had fallen into his eyes but he made no move to flick it away. He looked both older and impossibly young.

"Tim, please work with me. We'll make one last move and that will be it."

"No," he said. "I won't let you do this to me. I'm not leaving Twin Falls. I won't."

They stared at each other. She didn't know how to deal with his flat-out refusal. Maybe if she gave him some time...after all, they weren't going anywhere for a few months. He'd have an opportunity to cool down and they'd work this out the same as they always did.

"We'll talk more," Clare said. "It'll be okay."

He didn't answer her. She pulled his door gently closed.

THE NEXT MORNING, TIM WAS in his room, ignoring his alarm clock, waiting for her to come up and tell him he was going to miss the bus if he didn't get out of bed right now.

It was a routine that was both exasperating and comforting to her. She liked that he still needed her even as she simultaneously wished he didn't need her quite so much.

She let him sleep for another ten minutes and then went up. She knocked on his door but walked in because if he was really asleep, he wouldn't have heard her knock and if he was playing possum, listening to his iPod, he also might not have heard the knock.

He was not in the bed.

He was not in the bed and she told herself he was somewhere in the house but even as she ran for the bathroom, she knew it wasn't true. He said he wouldn't stay if she made him move to Seattle and Tim was nothing if not honest. He was a guy who followed through.

The bathroom, the family room, she opened the basement door and yelled for him, but he wasn't there. Even before she opened the hall closet...*boots, hat, coat, gone, gone, everything gone, thank God he's dressed warm, where could he go, where would he run*...she was already fumbling for the phone, pushing 911.

The dispatcher said they'd send a car over. She hung up and called Lindsey who was still asleep when she picked up the phone. Clare had a faint hope that he might have called Lindsey, but she hadn't heard from him.

When Clare told her what had happened, Lindsey grabbed her laptop and her purse and called an airport taxi from her landline while she asked Clare more questions and threw on her clothes. Clare should've told her not to come. It was expensive and she didn't even know how long Tim would be gone, maybe he was on his way home but she didn't say any of that because she didn't really believe it and she couldn't stand to be alone. "Hurry, Lindsey, please."

"I'm coming. Hang on."

When the police arrived, she had a picture of him on the table and another one set to go in a computer file. She didn't break down until the officer who'd been asking her the questions while his partner was upstairs in Tim's room told her she should call someone to come over and she realized there was no one she could call.

Her son was missing and she didn't know a single soul in Twin Falls to call to sit with her.

That wasn't true. She wanted Bryan. She just wasn't sure he'd come. Which wasn't true, either. He'd come. He would never make her endure this by herself. No matter what terrible things they'd said to each other, Bryan—sweet, generous, loyal Bryan—would come.

The police told her they were going to start searching for him and her first step was to call Tim's friends. She dialed Bryan's number. Allie and Bryan—Tim might have gone to them. Bryan wasn't used to being the full-time parent. He hadn't been around for Allie's playdate years. Maybe he didn't realize if a kid showed up on your doorstep you should call the parents. It could all be a mistake and she'd pretend to be mad that he didn't know these simple things, but she'd forgive him and Tim. She'd forgive everyone for everything if only Tim was there.

When she heard Bryan's voice, she started crying and she wasn't sure she was going to be able to stop. She needed to stop so she could ask if Tim was there and Bryan could reassure her that he had him.

"Tim's gone." She struggled to get those words out. "Is he with you?"

"Gone? What are you saying, gone?"

She gulped in a breath and steadied her breathing. "I think he ran away. Bryan, is he with you?"

"Oh, God. When?"

"Have you seen him?"

"No. I'm not home. I had to go into Dutton's headquarters for some meetings. I haven't been home in three days."

He hadn't seen Tim. The news settled in her stomach.

"Bryan, where would he go?" she said.

"You called the police?"

"They're here, but they're asking me to list places he might go and I can't. Where would a kid go in Twin Falls?"

"We'll find him, Clare. Hang on. I'll call Allie. My mom is here from South Carolina watching Allie for me, maybe he's there. I'll call you right back."

She held on to the phone, still crying softly.

"Clare, you need to hang up so I can call Allie. Who's there with you?"

"Two police officers. Um, one is named Mike. The other one is tall."

"Mike Avery, probably. He's a good guy. His daughter is a senior at the high school. Are they right there with you?"

She shook her head even though he couldn't see it. "No. I'm downstairs."

"I'm calling Allie. Go find Mike and stick with him until I call you back."

"I don't want to see them. I'll wait for you."

She hung up without letting him say goodbye. Then she stood, perfectly still, holding her phone and willing him to call back and tell her that Tim was safe with Allie. Maybe if she didn't go upstairs, didn't see the police, this could end right now the same way it began, with Tim and Allie. Please let him be with Allie. *Please let him be with Allie.*

Her phone rang.

"I'm sorry, she hasn't seen him."

She started to cry again.

"Clare, Clare, slow down. What happened?"

"We had a fight. About moving. I told him we were going to Seattle because I thought he wanted that but he said he wanted to stay here. He said he would run away, but I never… He doesn't even have anywhere to go."

"Okay. He'll probably come home on his own. He's mad, but he's not stupid. He might be headed your way now."

"This is Tim. He doesn't ever go halfway. He said he would leave and he did."

"All right, Allie's calling the kids on the team to check if any of them have seen him. He's somewhere and we'll find him."

"I wish you were here."

"I'm on my way. I'll be there as soon as I can. Promise."

She hung up and stood still. Bryan was coming. Lindsey was coming. They were going to get here as soon as they could. Then Tim would come home and everything would be fine. Tim would come home. He had to.

AFTER HE HUNG UP, Bryan called Mary and asked her to go over to Clare's house. His sister was good in a crisis and she knew everybody in Twin Falls. If Clare needed something, Mary would be able to help her.

Next, he called Allie back. His mom answered and she put Allie on.

"Are you doing okay, kiddo?"

"Is he really missing?"

"Seems that way," Bryan answered.

"Is he kidnapped?"

The word sent a chill through him. He bit the inside of his cheek.

"I hope not," he said. "Clare said they'd had a fight. She thinks he ran away. That's why it's super important for you to try to guess any place he might go or anyone he might call."

"He didn't call me," Allie said. Bryan heard the hurt in her words. He shared it. Tim could have called him. He'd have listened. He'd have tried to help. He still hadn't even processed the fact that Clare was moving to Seattle.

"He might. We don't know what he's doing."

"If he's not kidnapped, I hope he's not lost. He doesn't know about snow and frostbite and stuff. He wouldn't stay outside, would he, Dad?"

He reassured her with the same words he'd spoken to Clare. "He's a smart kid. We have to do what we can to find him, but in the meantime, we have to hope he's staying safe somehow. Okay?"

"Not really," she said. "Will you be here soon?"

"Another two hours," he answered.

"I wish you were here now. This sucks."

"We can stay on the phone as long as you want."

"I better call some more kids. I want to help."

"Call back if you want."

"I love you, Dad," Allie said.

"I love you back," Bryan answered. "Stay safe."

He'd had his meeting with Stan yesterday and it had gone better than he'd expected. Not only was Dutton going to chip in with a sponsorship for his skate school, but Stan wanted him to stay on as a consultant to train and mentor the sales force. He'd have to go to conferences a couple times a year, but the income would be welcome as he was getting the other business off the ground.

None of that mattered to him now. He pressed the accelerator. Clare needed him. He had to get to her.

THE MORNING WAS A BLUR. Shortly after she spoke to Bryan, Mary turned up at the front door. When Clare answered her knock, Mary pulled her into a hug and Clare let herself fall apart for just a minute. She pressed her face into the cold fabric of Mary's wool coat and cried.

She pulled herself together quickly, though, inviting Mary inside and setting her up at the dining room table with the middle-school phone directory. Clare went down the list of seventh graders and used a yellow highlighter to mark the name of any kid on the hockey team or in Tim's homeroom. She had a blue highlighter she used to mark off the names she'd heard him mention in passing—guys he ate lunch with, girls from his gym class, kids who rode his bus. Mary started calling the yellow names first, while Clare sought out the police officers. One had gone outside, while the other was still in Tim's room.

"We have his description and picture out on the Net, Ms. Sampson. All of our guys are looking for him and the surrounding departments have the information. We've got a lot of eyes watching for him."

"Thank you," she said, overwhelmed. "I was wondering what else I could help with."

"Could you look around here and make a list of what you think he might have taken with him?"

She grabbed a notebook off his desk and a pen. Looking around the familiar clutter of Tim's life, she had a moment of disassociation. She felt as if she were above, looking in, and she couldn't imagine how that woman down there had managed to lose her child.

She straightened her shoulders and squinted at the desk. She didn't have time for regrets now. She picked up the pen and wrote down *iPod*.

LINDSEY'S PLANE WAS grounded in Chicago. She called and said she was trying to rent a car.

Clare called Matteo, wishing he'd say Tim had reached out to him, but no luck. He said he'd head to the airport and try to fly standby. It would be at least a day before he'd make it in.

She hesitated before she called her dad. He'd become increasingly withdrawn and anxious in the past few years—she didn't want to upset him. But the local news was running Tim's picture and she didn't want her dad to hear that he was missing through some random mention on TV. He said he would go to church and start praying. At least he'd be around other people, she thought.

Danny showed, followed by John Langenforth and four minivans of hockey parents. They picked up flyers Mary had had printed and fanned out to start searching on foot. They were joined by the entire technical team from the bank, the manager with his suit pants tucked into tall snow boots, and as many tellers and loan officers as the office could spare.

Gusti's sent stacks of pizza at lunchtime and a deli delivery came, paid for by the hockey-referees club. The local grocery sent cases of water and a group of PTA parents brought the big coffee urns they used for meetings at school.

Allie called, her voice small and nervous, and asked if

she could help. She got the words out, but then a muffled sob escaped her and Clare thought it might be good for both of them if they waited together. When the girl came in, Clare took her hands and held them and she was surprised at how good it felt to have Allie with her. At that moment she felt as if Allie was sharing her worry, holding some of the fear. She hadn't had this experience before. Her worry had always been her own. She pulled Allie close and wrapped one arm around her shoulders, pressing a kiss on her hair.

"He's going to come back," Allie said. "He wouldn't want to leave for real. I know it."

Clare nodded. She hoped Allie was right.

The downstairs was crowded and people were constantly coming and going among the ringing of cell phones and police-radio static. Allie still looked shaken up so Clare said, "Want to come up to his room? Maybe you'll see something I missed."

She led the girl up and then closed Tim's door, thankful for the quiet. Allie turned a slow circle, looking at everything from the Sabres poster on the wall above the bed to the hamper with a week's worth of clothes spilling out.

"It's like he's here somewhere," Allie whispered. "Right?"

Clare's body went cold as she remembered that exact same feeling from the day of Gretchen's funeral. After the service and the graveside and the breakfast, she'd gone home with her parents and, still in her black dress, had walked into Gretchen's room. She'd realized at that moment that she was alone and would always be alone. She hadn't been able to imagine a future without Gretchen.

"He's somewhere, Allie," she said. "He'll be back."

"He told me one time that you're not like other moms. He said you're like his friend, and he could tell you stuff other kids don't tell their moms. He's probably mad, but he won't stay mad. He can't."

Allie took a step toward her and then they were holding each other and crying.

There was a soft tap on the door and Bryan walked in. He was tall and with the light behind him from the doorway, he looked beautiful. She held out one arm and he crossed the room in two strides, hugging her and Allie, holding them both while he told them it was going to be okay, everything would be okay.

Wrapped in his arms, held tight against his chest, she believed him. She believed him because Tim had been right all along and it wouldn't be fair if she didn't get a chance to tell him.

The last time she'd done this, standing in Gretchen's room, looking for evidence that her sister was still there, she'd been alone. She wasn't alone anymore. Bryan and Allie were here with her, feeling the same fear, the same hope, the same wrenching loss that she was. She'd done everything she could to make sure they didn't feel welcome, to keep them out of her life, but when she needed them, they'd been here without a question.

She needed them and they needed her right back.

All her life she'd refused to look for a home, but she'd found one anyway.

"I'm so glad you're here," she said. Allie and Bryan tightened their arms and held on.

Now all they needed was Tim.

If life were a movie, they would have found him at that moment. Maybe he'd have been locked in the garage or asleep in someone's spare bedroom all along. They'd have hugged and ruffled his hair and it would have been over.

The afternoon dragged on with no word.

More TV cameras showed up. She stood on the porch and listened as the Twin Falls police chief confirmed that they had found Tim's tracks. He'd left sometime before dawn, on foot, and based on what Clare had been able to tell them, he'd taken a bag containing some food and a change of clothes. He described what Tim had been wearing. They flashed pictures of his iPod and his cell phone and his Twin Falls hockey jacket even though half the people out searching had the exact same jacket.

A reporter asked how long he could stay alive if he was outside in these conditions.

The chief reiterated that they were lucky the day had warmed up and they had every hope they'd find him before dark.

Clare gave her statement, but she couldn't remember later what she said.

BRYAN WATCHED CLARE FROM the edge of the crowd. He had one arm around Allie. She hadn't left his side since he showed up. He felt guilty because he was so damn grateful he had his kid there to hang on to.

As he listened to the questions from the press and the chief's answers, he watched Clare's face. She was amazing. He knew how devastated she was, but she was on top of every detail, answered every question, did everything anyone asked her to. All of her energy was on finding Tim.

He pulled Allie closer.

She put her arms around his waist and held him tight. "You never gave Tim an autograph," she said. "When we find him, you have to sign his stick."

"You got it, kiddo."

"I'M NOT GOING TO suggest you sleep, Clare, but I'm letting you know that I'm here, if you want to take a break," Bryan said.

She was exhausted, but there was no way she could sleep. The tracking dogs had lost Tim's trail near the bus stop, but the driver didn't remember seeing him that morning and the security cameras hadn't picked him up. The police were wondering if he'd gotten in a car with someone. His cell phone hadn't been on since the day before. There was no data available to tell them if he was even still in Twin Falls or if he was on the move. She couldn't stop worrying—one situation more horrible than the last kept running through her mind. If she closed her eyes...the things she imagined...she was better off staying up.

"I'm glad you're here," she said.

The house was quieter than it had been earlier. The search was on hold until first light the next day. Two police officers were still in the dining room, one had a laptop open and the other was scanning printouts. She didn't have any idea what he was looking for, just felt a blind hope that he'd find something, that someone would find something, that would lead them to Tim.

They'd persuaded Allie to go up to sleep in the guest room about an hour ago.

Clare wished she could rest.

"Do you have your car?" she asked Bryan. "I can't

sit here anymore. If we drive around, maybe we'll see something or...I don't know. I need to be moving."

"Sure," he said. "Let me tell Allie I'm going."

"She's asleep."

"I don't want her to wake up and miss us. She's a heavy sleeper. I'm sure she'll drop right off again."

She got her coat and gloves and told the police officers she was going out, while Bryan went up to Allie. Suddenly he was yelling for her and then he and Allie were both running down the stairs.

"What?" she said. "What is it?"

"He texted Allie. She was asleep and didn't hear it." Allie handed the phone to Clare. "I woke her up to tell her we were going and she checked her messages."

Clare stared at the screen. "He's at the rink? We checked there. We went all through there."

The officer at the table closed his laptop. "I'll call it in. We'll get someone over there to open the door."

"I have a key," Bryan said. "Danny gave it to me so I could skate with Allie after hours."

Clare rushed ahead of them to the car. Allie flew past him and Bryan yelled to the cop behind that they'd meet him there.

The drive was less than ten minutes, but Clare thought she'd die before they made it. Bryan stopped the car outside the front door and the three of them ran up the steps.

"Tim!" Clare called while she banged on the doors. "Tim, are you there?"

Bryan unlocked the door and held it open for her and Allie. The swirling lights of the police car played across their faces as they pushed past him.

"Tim!" Clare yelled again. "Where are you?"

Light shone out of the door of the party room. They raced over and there he was. Clare stopped in the doorway when she saw his face.

"I'm sorry, Mom," Tim said. "I'm sorry I scared you, but I'm still not going home. I want to stay in Twin Falls. I'm going to—"

Allie had ducked past Clare and punched Tim in the shoulder. "You're being a jerk."

"You're not supposed to punch people anymore." Tim rubbed his shoulder.

"I wouldn't have to punch you if you didn't scare us half to death and make us worry all day and night about you!"

One of the police officers clicked on his radio. "He's safe," he said before backing out of the room.

Clare put her hands on Allie's shoulders, her eyes on Tim. "It's okay, Allie. I'll talk to him."

Bryan drew Allie aside and started to leave the room.

"Wait," Clare said. "Please." She drew in a deep breath. "I'm sorry, Tim. You've been asking me for something that's entirely reasonable to want. A home. People to love and people who love you. Friends you can grow up with. I thought I had good reasons for saying no to those things, but I was wrong. There's no reason not to want all that and more."

Tim pushed his hair out of his eyes. "So we can stay?"

"We can stay."

He flung himself into her arms and she held him and sent a thank-you up to heaven that she'd been given the gift of her son back, safe and whole. Not every parent got this gift. She needed to remember more often how much good fortune she had in her life.

"I hung up the collage," he said. She raised her head and noticed that he had finished the project. It was stunning. The images he and Allie had chosen and the way they'd arranged them gave the room energy and life. It was so very clearly the work of those two unique minds.

"It looks tremendous."

"Amazing," Bryan said.

She hadn't forgotten he was there.

She squeezed Tim and then released him. "Would you mind waiting outside the door with Allie for a minute? Right outside the door?"

He nodded.

"I'll watch him," Allie said. She clutched his T-shirt as they walked out the door.

Bryan bent and rubbed his knee. "I slipped coming in from the parking lot." She suspected he was trying to avoid eye contact with her.

"I can never tell you how much it meant to have you and Allie with me today," she said. "Or yesterday, I guess."

"I'm glad Tim is okay."

She nodded.

"You're really staying?" he asked.

"The strangest thing happened," she said. "I've been so sure that to keep myself and Tim safe we had to keep to ourselves. But then, on the worst day of my life, the only way I stayed sane was to hang on to you. You saved me."

"I love you."

"That right there still scares me," Clare admitted. "But I want to hear it more."

He stepped forward and she met him halfway. He put his arms around her, tugging her in until she was tight against his chest where she could feel every inch of him and know he was hers to keep.

"I love you." His voice rumbled up under her cheek. She kissed his neck.

"I love you," he said again.

"Again," she whispered.

"I love you."

His lips met hers as he said the last word and they kissed.

"I love you," he said, his lips moving against hers. "I want to spend my life loving you."

"Are you asking me to marry you?"

He smiled. "You'll know when I propose," he said. "That wasn't it, but you need to brace yourself, because it's coming sooner or later."

"I'll need to practice letting you love me."

He spread his hands and stroked down her body, cupping her bottom and lifting her to him. "I can help with that."

"I love you, Bryan," she said, the words coming so easily she wondered that it had taken her so long to say them. "I love you like crazy."

"Crazy is okay with me. Just make sure you keep it up."

She kissed him again, slow and sweet, savoring this amazing man under her hands, next to her body. She couldn't wait to get started learning every inch of his body and his heart.

* * * * *

COMING NEXT MONTH

Available November 9, 2010

LARGER-PRINT BOOKS!
GET 2 FREE LARGER-PRINT NOVELS PLUS
2 FREE GIFTS!

HARLEQUIN®

Super Romance®

Exciting, emotional, unexpected!

YES! Please send me 2 FREE LARGER-PRINT Harlequin® Superromance® novels and my 2 FREE gifts (gifts are worth about $10). After receiving them, if I don't wish to receive any more books, I can return the shipping statement marked "cancel." If I don't cancel, I will receive 6 brand-new novels every month and be billed just $5.44 per book in the U.S. or $5.99 per book in Canada. That's a saving of at least 13% off the cover price! It's quite a bargain! Shipping and handling is just 50¢ per book.* I understand that accepting the 2 free books and gifts places me under no obligation to buy anything. I can always return a shipment and cancel at any time. Even if I never buy another book from Harlequin, the two free books and gifts are mine to keep forever.

139/339 HDN E5PS

Name _____ (PLEASE PRINT) _____

Address _____ Apt. # _____

City _____ State/Prov. _____ Zip/Postal Code _____

Signature (if under 18, a parent or guardian must sign)

Mail to the **Harlequin Reader Service:**
IN U.S.A.: P.O. Box 1867, Buffalo, NY 14240-1867
IN CANADA: P.O. Box 609, Fort Erie, Ontario L2A 5X3

Not valid for current subscribers to Harlequin Superromance Larger-Print books.

**Are you a current subscriber to Harlequin Superromance books
and want to receive the larger-print edition?
Call 1-800-873-8635 today!**

* Terms and prices subject to change without notice. Prices do not include applicable taxes. N.Y. residents add applicable sales tax. Canadian residents will be charged applicable provincial taxes and GST. Offer not valid in Quebec. This offer is limited to one order per household. All orders subject to approval. Credit or debit balances in a customer's account(s) may be offset by any other outstanding balance owed by or to the customer. Please allow 4 to 6 weeks for delivery. Offer available while quantities last.

Your Privacy: Harlequin Books is committed to protecting your privacy. Our Privacy Policy is available online at www.eHarlequin.com or upon request from the Reader Service. From time to time we make our lists of customers available to reputable third parties who may have a product or service of interest to you. If you would prefer we not share your name and address, please check here. ☐

Help us get it right—We strive for accurate, respectful and relevant communications. To clarify or modify your communication preferences, visit us at www.ReaderService.com/consumerschoice.

HSRLP10R

*See below for a sneak peek from
our inspirational line, Love Inspired® Suspense*

*Enjoy this heart-stopping excerpt from
RUNNING BLIND
by top author Shirlee McCoy,
available November 2010!*

*The mission trip to Mexico was supposed to be an
adventure. But the thrill turns sour when Jenna Dougherty
and her roommate Magdalena are kidnapped.*

"It's okay. I'm here to help." The voice was as deep as the
darkness, but Jenna Dougherty didn't believe the lie. She
could do nothing but lie still as hands slid down her arms,
felt the rope around her wrists.

"I'm going to use a knife to cut you free, Jenna. Hold
still."

The cold blade of a knife pressed close to her head before
her gag fell away.

"I—" she started, but her mouth was dry, and she could
do nothing but suck in air.

"Shhh. Whatever needs to be said can be said when
we're out of here." Nick spoke quietly, his hand gentle on
her cheek. There and gone as he sliced through the ropes on
her wrists and ankles.

He pulled her upright. "Come on. We may be on
borrowed time."

"I can't leave my friend," Jenna rasped out.

"There's no one here. Just us."

"She has to be here." Jenna took a step away.

"There's no one here. Let's go before that changes."

"It's dark. Maybe if we find a light…"

"What did you say?"

"We need to turn on the light. I can't leave until I know that—"

"What can you see, Jenna?"

"Nothing."

"No shadows? No light?"

"No."

"It's broad daylight. There's light spilling in from the window I climbed in through. You can't see it?"

She went cold at his words.

"I can't see anything."

"You've got a nasty bruise on your forehead. Maybe that has something to do with it." His fingers traced the tender flesh on her forehead.

"It doesn't matter *how* it happened. I'm blind!"

Can Nick help Jenna find her friend or will chasing this trail have Jenna running blindly again into danger?

Find out in RUNNING BLIND, available in November 2010 only from Love Inspired Suspense.